DEATH
ON THE
WEB

Tanya Bourton

authorHOUSE®

AuthorHouse™ UK
1663 Liberty Drive
Bloomington, IN 47403 USA
www.authorhouse.co.uk
Phone: 0800.197.4150

Published by AuthorHouse 03/14/2017

ISBN: 978-1-5246-3385-1 (sc)
ISBN: 978-1-5246-3384-4 (e)

Print information available on the last page.

This book is printed on acid-free paper.

CONTENTS

Other books by Tanya Bourton

The Plight of Nimara
Return to Nimara
A New Dawn for Nimara

For my dear Auntie Helena

CHAPTER ONE

The music burst into life as it reverberated off the walls of the theatre, while Emma twirled effortlessly across the stage. She executed each step with perfection because of the countless hours spent practicing in the studio above the theatre. Her heart thudded its own rhythm against her rib cage, due to a euphoric cocktail of nerves and excitement.

Her feet were sore and bruised and her empty stomach growled loudly. Luckily, the sounds were masked by the boom that resonated from the orchestra in the pit below. Nevertheless, it was here, on the stage, blinded by the many lights that radiated intense heat that she truly felt alive. The familiar odours of make-up, dusty costumes and sweat, reminded her that this was where she belonged. She was a dancer and the theatre was her home and always would be. Emma's face and movements expressed each emotion dictated by the music and she fully immersed herself into her dancing role.

Just a week previously, Emma could never have envisaged herself actually performing on the stage with the main part. Then suddenly, Sarah, who was initially chosen to take the lead role, was rushed into hospital with acute appendicitis. As she was hurriedly wheeled through the long, sterile corridors towards surgery, it was rumoured that she screamed more out of despair for missing the opportunity to dance than out of the excruciating pain that she was going through. In fact, she threw herself into such a blazing tantrum that it took the anaesthetist and a male nurse to stop her from lashing out, kicking and punching before they could put her to sleep.

Everyone knew that Emma should have been the obvious choice for the role. Not only was she more talented than Sarah but also because of her unwavering dedication towards ballet. Mrs. Charmers, the dance teacher was aware that Emma would learn all of the routines in time for the show. In truth, she suspected that Emma already knew them perfectly well. On many occasions she had caught her peering through the window whilst Sarah was practising. Her expression was always intense as she admired each pirouette and each pas de chat performed by Sarah, yet her eyes showed such sorrow and yearning for it to be her instead.

Now, here she was, her dream had come true and all eyes were fixed on her as she danced alone on the stage. The pity she felt for Sarah had vanished; this was her night.

All too quickly, the music rose to a dramatic crescendo that ended the performance and Emma paused in her final position. There was a moment of silence and all she could hear was the fast beat of her heart and her quick, short breathes. Then, like a sudden, torrential storm, the applause pelted down and the cheers thundered and echoed throughout the room. Lightning flashed within her very core; its energy pulsated through her veins, flickering static, causing the hair on her arms and neck to stand on end. She closed her eyes and breathed in deeply, allowing the moment to soak into her pores and become part of her forever.

The final curtain dropped and an immediate mad rush began back to the changing room. It was full of chaotic motion as the girls were forced to share a tiny space together. They pushed and shoved each other for a place next to one of the few mirrors dotted around the room. As they quickly changed out of their costumes, they accidently knocked into one another; ducked to escape a punch from a fist; moved their feet to avoid the tread of a heavy foot. It was hard to believe that these were the same girls that just moments ago, danced like delicate butterflies and admired for it by a stunned audience.

Emma managed to grab one of the stools that was facing a mirror. She blotted out the screeches and squabbling that went on around her and gazed at her own reflection. She loved the way the liquid eye-liner followed the shape of her eyes, gently flicking up at the ends to give her a mysterious, oriental look. The daringly red lipstick made her lips more defined and fuller and the blusher gave the impression of a much thinner face. She knew that the make-up had created an illusion but could not believe just how elegant and mature it made her look. Deciding to keep the make-up on until she got back home, Emma turned her attention towards the costume that she was wearing. As the sound of the orchestra continued to play inside her head, she hung the colourful, delicate material on the hanger and placed it on the rail along with all the other costumes. She ached to be back on the stage again, even though she was on it only a few minutes ago. She would have to wait for the next day for the matinee and sadly, the final performance in the evening. Picking up her bag that contained her ballet shoes, towel and make-up, she left the room quietly, leaving the other girls to continue with their bickering.

She ran through the brightly lit corridor, rushing past the many grinning faces that expressed their admiration for her performance that night. With barely a glance, Emma continued towards the back stage door where her parents were already waiting for her. She could not wait to see the reaction on their faces as they had no idea that she had the leading role. She wanted it to be a surprise. There were many times in the past week, when she felt a burning desire to tell them about her amazing news but managed to stay strong and determined from allowing her secret from slipping out of her mouth.

As soon as she reached her parents, she could see that keeping it from them was worth it. Her mother was drying tears of joy from her eyes and her father stood straight backed, brimming with pride. Her mother flung her arms around her and whispered shakily, 'You were just amazing sweetie. I am just... oh... so very proud of you.'

Hearing those words meant everything to Emma and she closed her eyes to prevent herself from crying. She hugged her mother all the more tightly.

Her father placed his hand gently on her shoulder and said, 'You could have told us that you had the main part. I don't know how you kept that to yourself.' His tone was jovial but the extent of his emotion was clear. 'I think that someone deserves a treat of her favourite meal, pizza,' smiling smugly at his daughter.

Emma released her grip on her mother and replied with great enthusiasm, 'I would really love that.' She was ravenous as she had not eaten all day. Dancing on a full stomach made her feel sluggish. Emma's mother disagreed with her daughter's abstinence from food at those times but she knew that it would be pointless to say anything about it.

As they all made their way to the car, Emma decided to run ahead, leaving her parents a little way behind. She was in a state of utter bliss and the adrenaline was still flowing through her body. She hummed the tune to her final dance of the night and at times fell into step with the beat, moving from arabesque to pas de chat.

Bounding into the car, Emma put the seatbelt on and as her father began reversing out of the parking space, she remembered that there was a packet of crisps in the boot and shouted, 'Stop!'

Her father hit the breaks sharply while her mother whirled round in a panic to see what was wrong and with a sense of alarm in her voice, she asked, 'What is it?'

'I need something from the boot. I won't be a moment,' Emma replied sheepishly, undoing her buckle.

Her mother muttered, 'Can't it wait?'

Bolting out of the car, Emma hesitated for a brief second to give her mother a cheeky grin before running to the back of the car. She opened the boot, grabbed the packet of crisps and slammed it shut again. At that moment she felt an intense pain that sliced through her legs and heard a loud crack.

Everything had suddenly gone white.

★

Even though it was twenty years since that horrific night, Emma was still haunted by its memories. She jolted in her sleep and whimpered. Each painful experience forced itself back into her dreams. White light flashed before her eyes and she was being wheeled through corridor after corridor. Through blurred vision, she could see the concerned face of a young female doctor who was holding her hand tightly and trying to soothe her while running along the side of the stretcher. Emma felt the agonising pain rip through her body and howled uncontrollably.

A white flash of light changed the scene. Her parents were seated by her hospital bed, their faces bruised from the accident. They were holding each other as they cried. The doctor, a different one this time was explaining that Emma would need extensive operations to prevent her from losing both of her legs.

Once more, there was a flash of white light and Emma woke up screaming and shaking. For a moment, she breathed heavily and then burst into tears. Once she regained her composure, she sat up and reached for the lamp on the bedside table and switched it on. Her wheelchair was waiting at the side of her bed and slowly, she eased herself into it. Before leaving the bedroom, Emma looked at a framed letter that hung on the wall. The night of the crash, one of the teachers from the Royal Ballet School was in the audience, watching

Emma's performance. She was always seeking talented dancers and she knew that she found a gem in Emma. There was no doubt in her mind that she deserved a place amongst the chosen few and could start the following year. The letter inviting Emma to join the school dropped on the doormat only a week after she had been told that she would never walk again.

Emma wiped a tear that spilled down her cheek. She was only fifteen years old at the time of the accident, a child who was carefree and full of youthful expectations for the future. It was cruel to think that a thirteen year old boy who took his father's car for a joy ride, could take away her dreams and ambitions forever. On that fateful night as she grabbed the crisp packet and closed the boot, the boy lost control of the car and smashed into her legs, crushing them between his bonnet and the boot of her parents' car.

An eyewitness said that at the moment of impact, the boy's face turned white and he bawled like a baby. The boy admitted later, that his tears were not from causing injury to her but from the fear of being caught. His father loved the car and would be very angry at him for crashing it. The court decided that it was an accident and as a young offender, he could only be cautioned. The boy could carry on with his life in the usual way whereas, Emma was left with nothing, not even a glimmer of hope that she would ever walk again let alone the very essence of her life, dance.

Here she was now; twenty years later, single, living in a small flat above a shoe shop in the centre of town and working in a supermarket just a street away. Her days normally started well, because the lift that barely had the space to fit the wheelchair, enabled her to get down to the ground floor but there was one occasion when it was broken and the shopkeeper had to carry her down the stairs. Emma found the experience humiliating and found it difficult to come to terms with the possibility that there could be times when she would need help.

Emma was living alone because she made a conscious decision to leave home upon reaching adulthood. Emma's parents begged her not to go but she felt that it was necessary because they were suffocating her with their love. She found them overwhelming and unbearable to live with. Their faces full of pity every time they looked at her. Emma wanted to prove not only to her parents but to herself as well that she could lead an independent life without the constant reminder that she is a cripple.

The buzzing sound of her mobile phone distracted her bleak thoughts and she picked it up out of curiosity. Emma wondered who could be texting her at that time of the morning? She saw that it was a notification from a new social network, 'Sanctuary'. For some unknown reason, in a moment of madness, she had decided to join the group a few months ago and forgot all about it until now. Pressing the button to open the site, she was intrigued to see that it was an invite from a person called Barry Dunmore, who claimed to have been in her year at school. Scrolling down, she came to an old photograph. It was instantly familiar to her. Twenty five pupils had been put into rows and made to smile for the camera. In the centre sat a balding, grey haired teacher, whose tie was slightly off centre. It made Emma smirk as she said, 'Mr. Robins.' This was a photograph of her tutor group at the start of the year; coincidentally she had just turned fifteen at that time.

Her eyes were drawn to a boy on the back row of the photograph who was not smiling. He was very large with rosy cheeks that were noticeable even at that distance where he was sitting. Barry Dunmore; the fat sweaty kid who everyone laughed at. Scrolling back to read the message, she was surprised to see that her name was amongst just four other individuals to be invited to a reunion. They were all asked to stay at his house in Dorset for a weekend.

Emma tapped the phone in the palm of her hand and looked around the room which was basic and bare, ironically reflecting her life. Since that fateful night, she had lost contact with everyone outside of her family. After the accident, her time was spent going back and forth to the hospital for the countless operations and then for tedious physiotherapy sessions. When Emma was well enough to go back to school, her parents thought it would be best for her to be tutored at home, however, she could not focus on the lessons and as a result failed to pass her exams. The only job that she could find was to work behind the till at a supermarket. She met lots of people and work mates but no one that she could call a friend and always returned to an empty flat.

Once more she gazed up at the framed letter and then without any more hesitation pressed the screen to accept the invite.

'Why not?' she said to herself. 'Perhaps I might even find a little excitement.'

CHAPTER TWO

Barry threw his keys carelessly on the kitchen counter. He barely heard the loud jangling noise they made as they smacked the marble top and slid a few inches before stopping. It had been a typical working evening into late night and the booming beat of the constant bass drum caused his ears to hiss annoyingly. Sighing, he opened the fridge door and let the refreshing cold air caress his hot and sweaty face. After a few moments, he pulled out a can of beer, snapped the ring pull and drank greedily, emptying the can in just a few gulps. Like magic, the liquid soothed his dry throat and numbed his aching muscles.

He thought back to the start of the evening when he was waiting by the front door to be greeted by the host of an extremely impressive house. While she approached to let him in, he watched her through the clear glass door as she sashayed towards it with a deliberate, sexy swagger. Her immediate expression at the sight of him suggested that she was thrilled to be getting her money's worth. Barry knew that he was attractive but it was not something that he felt smug about. His looks were not something that nature had provided him with when he was born. It took a lot of hard work to achieve it. He spent countless hours at the gym and had attended a few rather expensive dental appointments. Nevertheless, the results were worth it. His perfect straight, dazzling white teeth, six pack and pert bottom captured the eyes of many admirers. It also helped that he had a natural boyish smile that was both cheeky and yet bashful. He was taken by the host to the lounge where he was introduced to twenty, beautiful women sipping champagne. They were polite, perhaps even a little shy at first as they let their eyes roam over his sculptured body. Barry was a Butler in the Buff and although his friends laughed at this, it paid well. He occasionally earned extra money when he was asked to perform a seductive dance towards the end of the night. It was something that he felt obliged to do. However, he could get even more cash if he considered taking one or two eager women upstairs to the bedroom. He knew that a few of his fellow Butlers did this on a regular basis but he vowed never to sink that low.

After all the introductions to the beautiful guests were over, he was escorted to the large kitchen. Barry was surprised to see that all of the worktops were made of stainless steel. He felt that they would have been more suitable for a restaurant than a home. Four chefs were busy creating sumptuous delights for the women to graze on but everyone knew that what they really wanted was to feast on the Butlers. Barry was relieved to see that another two Butlers were also hired apart from him. As a professional, he knew how to handle these kind of women but being the only focus for so many hours would be exhausting.

As the party started to get into full swing, it never ceased to amaze him how women could change in a space of a few hours. The alcohol began to flow; stifled titters became raucous cackles, carefully selected words were rejected in favour of coarse language and perfect postures slumped. Before his very eyes, each princess turned into a hideous hag that revolted him. They all sat around the table forming a tableau of a witches' coven. As he served them, he was subjected to long nails scraping his arms, fingers pinching his bare bottom and wandering hands snaking up beneath his apron. His mind was sharp and his actions quick, enabling him to avoid too much contact.

The behaviour of the women at these parties was the cause of putting Barry off from ever wanting to form a relationship. Could he ever be sure what disgusting, lustful wench hid from behind the mask of deceit?

Taking another beer out of the fridge, Barry moved into the small lounge and sat on the old, comfortable settee. He took a sip of his beer and placed the can on the wooden coffee table before him. He sat back and looked around the room. The walls needed repainting and the carpet was worn but it was his home. He was proud that he managed to buy a terrace house just on the outskirts of London and sometimes found it rather ironic that he should end up living only a few streets away from his childhood home.

His eyes settled on a photograph on the side cabinet which made him grin. It was one of those portrait pictures that every child was forced to be in at school. He stared at the chubby face that attempted to smile back at him. Things had been so different back then. Nobody admired his looks, apart from his doting mother and loving aunt.

His mother was a short, rotund woman who had a pleasant face. Her movements were slow due to the large amount of weight that she had to carry. It seemed impossible for such a small frame to manage to hold so much fat but over time she expanded even further. However, she was quick witted, intelligent and very humorous. There were times when she made Barry laugh so much that he pleaded for her to stop as he could not breathe anymore. Her only weakness was food and her belief that it was essential to consume large amounts of it. 'You are a growing boy,' she often exclaimed proudly whilst piling another helping of pie and chips on Barry's plate.

In truth, he was a growing boy, but not so much in stature as in width. He was unable to do things that other boys took for granted. He would get a stitch after running up a few steps and left panting heavily. He could not go on a slide or a swing as his body was too big to fit into them. Being constantly ridiculed at school wore him down. He wished that the other children would accept him for who he was but soon discovered that life was not like that. In fact the bullying turned nasty the day he broke the chair during a maths lesson. As he sat down, the seat groaned loudly and slowly the legs began to give way. With a loud crash the chair collapsed and Barry tumbled to the floor. The buttons of his shirt burst open, flashing the rolls of fat that were hidden beneath it. His face burned like fire as the whole class roared with laughter. The teacher merely stood, dumbfounded. His arms were raised and his hands comically rested on his head. The only comment he made was, 'You actually broke the chair.'

What troubled him the most during those times was how his mother was becoming more and more ill. The moment the doctor diagnosed her as clinically obese, instead of trying to lose weight, his mother got it into her head that she would die. She chose not to change her ways and carried on feeding her illness all the more until her heart lost its fight.

Consumed by such sad memories, Barry drank the rest of the beer and went back into the kitchen to fetch yet another one. Just as he was about to grasp the can in his hand, he stopped, paused and took a small bottle of sparkling water from the fridge instead. He twisted the cap off and made his way back to the lounge.

His thoughts turned back to his mother and her funeral. He cried bitterly as they lowered her body into the ground. He shed tears of frustration; she did not have to die in that way. If only she had a strong will and ate less. His heart pained with the loss and his mind spun with the sudden realisation that he was heading in the same way.

Seeing his despair, Aunt Lucy moved hastily towards him and flung her arms around him. She tried to soothe him as he whispered, over and over again, 'Help me… help me… help me.'

Barry placed the bottle on the table and settled into a more comfortable position. His thoughts swiftly moved on to the happy times that he spent with his aunt. It would bring some kind of relief from the dark mood that he was now in. After his mother died, he went to live with Aunt Lucy who lived in a quaint house in Dorset, shrouded by woodland. Beyond the woods was a blanket of fields. Barry had never seen so much green and so much sky before and felt that he could physically breathe more easily now that he was away from the smog and grime of London. He grew to love the place and very quickly settled in to the new surroundings and changes in his life.

His aunt was the total opposite of his mother. She was of average height and very slim. Her movements were quick and she was full of vitality and her love of life was contagious. She had time for everything and swept through the house like wildfire as she cleaned every nook and cranny until the place sparkled. It always had a fresh smell of country air and detergents. Her conversation always ended on a positive note and she took great interest in Barry's thoughts and opinions on different subjects.

Slowly, self-belief crept inside his mind and nestled in a less darkened corner. Once it grew strong enough, it leapt and attacked his feelings of worthlessness that had thrived on the many years of mental and physical bullying. There was only one similarity that his aunt had with his mother and that was for the love of food. However, she preferred to serve fresh vegetables and fruit, claiming that it was important to nourish the body with the appropriate vitamins and minerals. Barry was fascinated by the various shapes and colours that were placed on his plate and enjoyed the different flavours that were all new to him. He was enthralled to see his weight melt away. With each pound he shed, the more energetic he became. He felt truly alive and content.

Then suddenly, Barry's smile disappeared when his thoughts moved on another two years to when he was given the most devastating news. Something that he had to face alone. There was no devoted aunt that he could turn to for comfort. A tear welled up in his eyes and he tried to blink it away. He tried hard to drive the bad memory from his mind but it was futile. Like all bad recollections, they have the habit of being relived again and again. Barry was seventeen and doing extremely well at college. He was popular with the lads who admired him and the girls that adored him. He had just returned from the final class of the day, burst through the front door and called out cheerfully, 'Auntie, I'm back.' But all that followed was silence. Frowning, Barry put his bag down and made his way nervously into the lounge. His auntie was sitting in the arm chair facing the window. She was completely motionless. On closer inspection, Barry could see that she had been crying. Her eyes were puffed and red rimmed. Her lips were still slightly quivering. 'Auntie?' he questioned as the feeling of dread clawed his throat.

Slowly, his aunt turned towards him and held out her shaking hands. Without question, Barry went towards her and grabbed them into his and knelt before her. He said nothing but gazed wide-eyed as if searching her face for any clue or sign for the reason that caused her distress. The few words that she muttered punched him hard in the stomach and pierced his heart. 'It's cancer. There is nothing they can do.'

At that moment he closed his eyes and pursed his lips, giving them the appearance of a thin line. He could not believe how cruel life could be. It seemed that no sooner he lost his mother to one illness, he was about to lose his aunt to another.

As the cancer spread, his dear aunt's strength faded and so did her independence. Barry gave up college to take care of her. She feared going into hospital and wanted to remain at home. She looked after him when he needed her the most and brought back happiness into his life. It was now his opportunity to show her how much he loved her and appreciated her devotion. He was determined to let her have her wish to die at home, with the dignity that she deserved and the knowledge that she was truly loved. His aunt preferred to stay downstairs during the day and go back to her bedroom at night. On many occasions as he carried her back and forth, she would look up at him sadly and say, 'You are so good and patient with me but I should be looking after you.' Barry would just smile and kiss her gently on the forehead and whisper, 'You did more than that for me.'

Three months later, Aunt Lucy passed away peacefully in her sleep as Barry held her hand. Silent tears cascaded down his pale face the moment she released her final breath. Heartbroken, he watched as her tiny, frail body was taken away to be placed in the chapel of rest. Broken, barely knowing what to do, he walked around the house going into each of the rooms. Without her presence, the house was an empty shell. The clock on the kitchen wall still ticked and the annoying stray cat scratched the wooden fence outside. The moon continued to light the night sky and the gentle breeze rustled the golden, autumn leaves. The world carried on moving and yet Barry felt that it had stopped, leaving a gaping hole inside of him. The next day, he joined the local gym to release the anger and sorrow that he was feeling from the pit of his stomach. He punished his body; tortured his muscles until he almost dropped from exhaustion. From then on, Barry went to the gym every day and soon his thin, wiry body became toned with well-defined muscles. This helped him to find a job that paid well in London and at the age of 21, he packed his bags and moved to a fresh new life away from the sad memories that the house contained.

Barry picked up the bottle of water from the table and quickly finished it to the last drop. As he placed it onto the table, his eyes fell on his mobile phone. He reached for it and automatically opened his page on the new social network site, 'Sanctuary', which he had recently joined. He had made no specific contacts as yet but noticed that some of the names on it were familiar to him. After moving to Dorset, he had lost all contact with anyone from his old school and to be honest, never wanted to. There were times, however, when he wondered how some of them would react to the new and improved version of Barry Dunmore. Perhaps some of them had not aged well and had grown fat or bald. That would be a kind of justice that would satisfy him immensely after what they put him through. Perhaps it was about time that he confronted them and show what he had become. Part of him still shivered at the thought of coming face to face with the hardcore bullies but he would like to know how certain members of his tutor group were getting on. What became of Emma, after her terrible car accident? Did she ever walk again?

For some time, he toyed with the idea of inviting some of them to his aunt's house in Dorset. She had left it and all her worldly possessions to him in her will. It seemed insane, but why not? Pressing the buttons quickly, he selected Emma Sanders, Sarah Fletcher, Jim Denver, Danny Acker and Rachael Tanner and typed a brief message to each of them. It read, 'Barry Dunmore would like to invite you to a weekend reunion of a few school friends. Friday 27th November, 8pm. R.S.V.P!' Once they were all sent, all that he could do was wait and see if anyone would reply. Just as he placed his phone on the table, it beeped. To his astonishment the first reply had already come through. It was from the beautiful, dancing Emma that he secretly fantasised about and cried when he heard the news of her accident. He sat back and sighed and wondered if perhaps this could be a good omen. Surely only good things could come from reunions. With sudden enthusiasm, Barry made a promise to himself. He would make sure that this was going to be a weekend to remember.

CHAPTER THREE

'Believe me, this is one of a kind. I don't print my art work.' Sarah could feel herself losing control as her voice started to rise with exasperation. The Town Hall was full of people, milling around the various stalls. Craft fairs were usually an enthralling experience. You met so many interesting individuals who were either browsing, genuinely interested in your work or just in need of a conversation. However, there was nothing enthralling about today. Sarah was standing behind a table surrounded by many examples of her most recent art work. The painting to her left was of a romp of otters, typically at play and splashing excitedly in the water. One of the otters appeared to be glancing out of the picture with a look of sympathy on its face. Without doubt, she was a very talented artist. The otters looked so lifelike that it would not have surprised anyone if they suddenly jumped out of the canvas and ran away.

Sarah was holding up a large painting and staring wide-eyed at a tall, well-built, middle-aged woman, who was scrutinising the picture over her nose. Her wrinkled, weather-beaten face was scrunched up and her lips squeezed together in disgust.

'I am sure that I saw this in the local charity shop just the other day.' The woman spoke with a shrill voice which was heavily punctuated with sarcasm. She then squinted and thrust her head forward causing lines to appear on her neck that reminded Sarah of a turkey. 'Their legs look bandy and their eyes are all wrong.'

Sarah took a deep breath and managing to retain her composure, informed the irritating woman, 'These are wild horses caught in mid-gallop. It expresses their strength and agility as noble creatures.'

'I can see that they are horses perfectly well,' said the woman and moved back into her original position, 'and I did see this picture at the local charity shop for one pound fifty!'

Sarah deliberately took her time to place the painting back on its stand in order to have time to regain her self-control. She faced the woman directly and leaning forwards, placed her hands on the table. Interpreting this as a confrontational gesture, the woman flinched and took a small step back. Seeing this, Sarah smiled, slightly feeling satisfied with her small victory and then asked her in a slow, menacing voice, 'What exactly are you trying to imply here?' The sense of control gave her more confidence. 'Are you insinuating that I am a fraud?'

The woman glared uneasily at Sarah but remained adamant. She folded her arms and stood as straight as possible. 'Yes, I do indeed suggest that you are a fraud. You did not paint any of these pictures. I suspect you buy copies cheaply and then sell them as your own work for a profit.'

Sarah's mouth fell open with disbelief. She had not expected such a serious accusation.

The woman continued smugly, 'You do not fool me one bit. A person like you with your velvet skirt and floppy hat could never understand the techniques of fine brush work. Even so, having said that, these pictures are not that good.'

Sarah felt anger surge through her entire body. She pressed her lips firmly together in order to try and keep her rage under control. Her face was on fire, burning crimson and then flaring into hot white. Her rage was at bursting point and nothing was going to hold it back any longer. In one huge explosion, Sarah's words spewed out like lava, 'How dare you... you... stupid woman! Can't you see this?' She flung her arm out and pointed to the painting. 'It's paint? P-A-I-N-T, PAINT! How thick are you? Copies are smooth... understand? Am I making myself clear? Go back to buying your things from the charity shop, you cheapskate and leave me alone. Besides, I love my floppy hat!'

Running out of steam, her rant came to an abrupt end. She stood panting; her nose was still flared and her nails dug into the palms of her hands. Slowly, she became aware that it was deadly silent. She took her eyes off the annoying woman and glanced around the room. Everyone was staring at her. Some of the stallholders were grinning, pleased that she had the guts to do what they sometimes felt like doing. The shoppers were clearly on the woman's side as they looked at her icily. They made her feel like a vulgar insect that had just crawled out of a hole. They would not be going to her stall anytime soon that was for sure.

The woman merely tutted and then with a final flourish announced, 'I am sure that they can texture prints nowadays.' She had to have the final word and whirled around on her heels then sauntered towards the exit sign.

Once the show was over, everyone went back to their previous business and the room was filled once more with buzzing conversation.

Deflated, Sarah slumped down on the plastic chair and grabbed the chocolate bar that poked out of her bag. She ripped the wrapper off in one swoop, bit into it fiercely and began to chew aggressively. As she carried on eating, she thought to herself gloomily that this was not how it was meant to be and began to think back to where this had all started.

At the age of eighteen, after being rejected by all of the CDET accredited schools, she realised that she would never be a professional dancer. Although, it pained her greatly, she had to admit that she was not good enough and this caused her to wallow in self-pity for almost a year. She became grumpy and withdrawn, leaving her parents at a loss as to how they could make her happy again.

One evening, purely by chance, Sarah realised that she had a natural talent for drawing when her little sister, Katie entered her room without knocking and sat on the floor. She was holding an exercise book, sheets of plain paper and a couple of pencils and stared at Sarah with such a look that only a child knows how to give. Even though Sarah was particularly feeling sorry for herself that day, she could not ignore her sister. 'Okay Munchkin, what is it?' Sarah asked managing a smile.

Her sister told her that there was a school project that had to be completed by the next morning and she could not draw a lion properly no matter how much she tried. To stop her from moaning, Sarah took the pencils and paper and agreed to give it a go but first she made her sister promise never to enter the room without knocking again. Once she started to draw, she became so focused that she was not aware of anything else apart from the image of the lion that slowly took form on the paper. When she was finally satisfied that the drawing was complete, it was already dark outside and way past her sister's bedtime. Sarah found her sister curled up on the floor with her thumb in her mouth. Gently, she tapped her on the shoulder and showed her the drawing. When her sister saw it, she screamed with joy and with a sudden burst of energy, ran to show her parents. They gasped in awe and very quickly pushed her into joining a local art group where she began to experiment with oils. It was not long before her friends asked her to do commissioned work for them which stirred the notion of fame in Sarah's mind. She dreamed of seeing her work hanging on the walls of the most elite galleries with hordes of people gathering round to admire her masterpieces. Yet here she was, twenty years later, being insulted in a Town Hall by an amateur critic.

'Chocolate? And there was I thinking you were on yet another diet.' Sarah recognised the voice instantly. It was Jim Denver, the only person that she had stayed friends with since leaving school. He was well spoken and yet, at times, a slight cockney accent crept through.

'You always turn up just when I don't want to see you,' she answered, pretending to be annoyed with him. In fact, she was always pleased to see him. Just by being there, he had a way of making her feel so much better about things. It was clear that they adored each other and Sarah had to admit to herself that if it was not for the fact that Jim had the same taste in men as she did, there could have been a romantic relationship between them. However, due to his sexual preference, their intimacy would have to remain purely on a plutonic basis.

Jim carefully manoeuvred through the meticulously arranged paintings and sat down in the vacant chair next to Sarah. The scent of freshly washed hair and the subtle undertone of cologne wafted across to her. It was a pleasant smell that Sarah took pleasure in sniffing. Today it was even more pleasing as it took the edge away from the nasty smell of damp and chip fat that spread around the room from the café.

Jim always looked stylish in his fashionable clothes that fitted him perfectly due to his slim physique. His jeans were more smart than casual and complimented his shirt and suit jacket. Sarah was amused by the peach handkerchief tucked into his jacket's top pocket. Peach was this season's colour and Jim took pride in his up-to-date knowledge of the fashion scene.

'Sold many?' Jim enquired nodding towards a painting to his left.

Sarah glared at him in response.

'Hmm, not today then.' He raised his eyebrows comically but his tone was one of disappointment. He hated to see his friend so deflated and felt it was unfair that she had to go through the same set back again and again. He was concerned that one day this would wear away her enthusiasm and passion for art. It would be such a tragedy if she closed the paint box, put away the easel and gave up on her dream. Jim decided to divert the conversation. 'Hey, what did you think of that invite from Barry?'

Sarah frowned still seething about the nasty woman.

'You know, the one on Sanctuary that was sent at three in the morning for crying out loud,' Jim said impatiently, 'my phone buzzed and it woke me up.'

Realising what Jim was talking about, Sarah answered, 'Oh God yes. That was weird. A bit creepy, don't you think? After all this time, inviting a few chosen people from his school days. We weren't even friends with that lot. Just in the same tutor group.'

Jim shrugged his shoulders and took his mobile phone out of his jeans pocket. He held it in his hands, barely looking at it. After a moment of silence he commented, 'Emma has already accepted the invite. Remember Emma, the girl who took your place when you had your appendix removed?' He suddenly grinned at the memory of visiting Sarah in hospital. She threw an apple at him when he told her that the show didn't matter. He had failed to duck in time and ended up with a lump on his forehead. When Sarah realised what she had done, the look on her face was priceless. Her jaw dropped and her eyes grew wide. Her hands clutched the sides of her face and she shook her head in horror. He lost count of how many times she apologised.

'Of course I remember Emma. That awful accident.' Sarah lowered her head sorrowfully.

Still pursuing the subject of the invite, Jim asked hopefully, 'Are you going?'

Sarah gasped, 'What, for a freaky weekend with people I haven't seen for years?' She was astonished that Jim would even have to ask.

Once again, Jim paused for a moment and then quietly murmured, 'It could be fun.'

Sarah chose to ignore him and seeing this, Jim pressed further, 'I'll look after you.'

Sarah sighed but a smile started to form on her lips. She always gave in to him, 'OK, I'll go but you're driving.'

Jim punched the air happily and then trying to reassure her replied, 'Of course, no problem. I'll drive. It will be fun, you know.'

For some strange reason, Sarah could not shake off the sense of foreboding that she was feeling about going to the reunion. She had always trusted her instinct and in most cases it served her well. This did not feel right at all and that worried her.

Unaware of Sarah's thoughts, Jim took her bag and started to fish around inside of it until he pulled out her phone. 'We should accept the invite now, just in case you change your mind.' He turned to look at her and seeing the doubt in her eyes, hesitated for a brief moment and then opened her Sanctuary application and said, 'In fact, I'll do it.'

Just watching him pressing the screen to send the message made her shiver. She felt nervous and wished that for once she had said no to him.

CHAPTER FOUR

Barry stopped the car just before the large, white gates that led to the spacious driveway. He gazed at the house nestled snugly between the stone walls that surrounded it. The walls were decorative and appeared to embrace the house as if protecting it from harm. Whenever Barry returned, he found himself feeling astounded by its beauty. It was undeniably grand and yet welcoming.

The whole house had recently been painted and the roof re-tiled by contractors that Barry hired and yet the garden, in sharp contrast, was clearly neglected. Aunt Lucy used to lovingly dedicate a lot of her time and effort into the garden so that it always looked perfect. He smiled to himself as he visualised her pottering around, inspecting each flower. She wore a straw sun hat even during the colder months and thick, green gardening gloves. A humungous watering can swung by her side as she lugged it around with difficulty. Aunt Lucy did this even when the soil was wet enough to sustain the foliage. Red and yellow roses climbed up the front wall of the house, creating an enchanting archway that framed the door. A variety of shrubs stood proudly as though guarding the many flowers that were carefully arranged around them. In the centre of the garden was a magnificent fountain that continuously surged the water up with such force that it reached high in the air before tumbling down heavily to the ground. Even though it made a loud noise, it was soothing. In a quieter corner was a pond with a miniature bridge over it which was decorated with small flowers that dipped, stroking the lily-pads that bobbed on top of the water. Beneath the lily-pads, Koi carp often clustered together or broke away from the rest, energetically darting to and fro. He never really cared about the garden but always felt in awe as it flourished by the mere touch of his aunt's gentle hands.

Slowly, Barry's smile disappeared as the image of his aunt faded away like a ghostly apparition that soon completely vanished together with the flowers, shrubs, fountain and pond. All that remained was the long grass and weeds that desperately needed attention. Barry lowered his eyes in shame. When his aunt became ill, he tended the garden just to please her. When it was too cold, he would place her in the armchair that faced the window overlooking the garden. She loved to watch or advise him on what to do; making sure that he was looking after it properly. When it was warm he would put her into the wheelchair so that she could settle in her favourite spot by the pond and enjoy the glory of nature. Those were the times she loved the best. She would often close her eyes and breathe in deeply the scent from the freshly mowed lawn and the various aromas from the plants and shrubs and listen silently to the splashing of the water. Barry was pleased that he managed to give her a little joy.

After Aunt Lucy died, Barry no longer had the incentive to look after the garden. His heart was no longer in it. He sold the fountain that constantly had to be cleaned and got rid of the fish because they were too high maintenance for him. The flowers merely withered away from neglect. After moving to London, his visits were few and the gaps between each one widened. The house no longer felt like his home. It was cold and empty and lost its appeal.

Taking a deep breath, he stepped out of the car and swung the heavy, creaking gates open. Quickly, he returned to his car and drove through them and onto the driveway. Once parked, he made his way to the front door and calculated that there was enough space for five more cars. Even if all of his guests chose to drive their own car, there would be enough space to accommodate them.

Fishing out his keys from his jacket pocket, he suddenly stopped and frowned. Something was not quite right with the front door. Something was missing. For a few moments he stared at it, trying to remember what it might be. Then, suddenly, it dawned on him; the horseshoe was no longer hanging on the nail just above the knocker. Searchingly, he looked down on the ground but it was not there. It had hung on that nail for over forty years and no matter how vile the weather, it never fell off. He then noticed it, hidden behind the drainpipe and picked it up. After all these years it was a little rusty but otherwise in good condition. He shrugged his shoulders and opened the door. As he walked inside, he promised himself that he would hang it back later. He was not a superstitious man but his aunt loved that horseshoe and well... it had always been there.

The inside of the house was as neglected as the garden, if not more so. The air was stale as the windows had remained closed for at least three years. A few cobwebs hung from the ceilings and a thick layer of dust coated every surface. It never endingly mystified Barry that even though the house was completely empty, dust still managed to form with such density.

Finding himself in the lounge, his eyes were automatically drawn to the space by the window. He had deliberately removed the armchair but in his mind he could still see his aunt sitting there with red and puffy eyes and lips that trembled. He tried to swallow hard in order to hold back the tears but subconsciously whispered, 'Auntie?' The feeling of dread clawed at his throat in the same way it had done on that dreadful day.

He went from room to room; each one holding a different memory. The kitchen was where his aunt baked his favourite cake; the study was where they both played computer games together; the bathroom was where he had his first shave and cut himself badly in the process. His aunt made a fuss and tried to stop the bleeding. When the panic was over she tried to advise him on the best way of doing it. Barry did love this house, even though the many happy times were overshadowed by his aunt's illness and death.

As he looked around, he became convinced that holding the reunion here was a good idea. In a way it was rather ironic. This was the place that gave him the opportunity to run away from the kids that bullied him. Now this was going to be the place where he would stop running and face all of his past demons and come to terms with his more recent bereavement by confronting them. He decided to stay and clean the place up himself. It was his responsibility and he was determined to do things properly.

The electricity had to be reconnected and the water turned back on. He hoped that everything was still in working order as nothing had been used since his aunt passed away. Some of the household items would have to be replaced because they were either sold or in bad condition.

His attention was drawn back to the horseshoe that he had placed on the lounge table. He picked it up and studied it closely. He felt its heavy weight in his hand and rubbed the jagged edges that were formed by icy winds and rain. If he truly wanted this house to feel like his property, he needed to put his own stamp on it. Without any thought or a moment's hesitation, he threw the horseshoe into the bin. It made a heavy thud as it hit the bottom but Barry barely noticed. This was the start of the many changes that he would make to the house. Barry had enough money tucked away in his savings account to make all the necessary modifications according to his own personal taste. He was now focused and rather excited by the prospect of redecorating each room. There was plenty to do and yet so little time left to do it in. The reunion was only a few weeks away. He would have to hire a skip and just like the horseshoe, get rid of the unwanted items. He was pleased that he had something to occupy his mind, at least for now.

CHAPTER FIVE

Rachael dashed down the stairs in a state of panic into the kitchen where the fire alarm was blaring angrily. Taking the mop from the utility room, she raised it towards the ceiling, stretching herself as much as she could. Finally, Rachael managed to poke the tiny alarm button, switching it off. She paused for a second, and then made haste towards the oven after detecting the smell of burnt cheese. Rachael had been pre-occupied with the ironing, forgetting about the lasagne that she was cooking for dinner. Whilst opening the oven door, she automatically glanced at the clock on the wall. It was already six o'clock and Danny would be home in fifteen minutes.

Danny was always punctual. His whole life was governed by the clock. When the two of them started dating, Rachael quickly realised that she would have to accept this if she wanted to remain with him. However, she realised the full extent of his quirkiness once she moved into his house. Everything she did had to fit into his schedule. He would rise at five-thirty every morning to get ready for work. Rachael would get up before him to prepare his breakfast and have it ready on the table as he entered the room. She also had to make sure that his attaché case containing his packed lunch together with his shoes, that she polished every morning, were always ready for him by the front door when he left for work at precisely seven o'clock. Rachael had to follow a similar ritual at the weekend when he would still leave the house at the same time but instead of going to work he would go for a long run in the nearby park. Rachael had to replace his shoes for trainers and have a bottle of chilled, still mineral water ready for him to take.

Whilst Danny was out, Rachael spent her time cleaning the house from top to bottom as he insisted that a clean house was a happy house. Busy or not, she would have to keep her eyes on the time as the dinner had to be on the table at six-thirty. Weekends, lunch would have to be served at 1 p.m. Rachael could never relax, she was always on edge. There were times, especially when she felt exhausted and at her lowest, Rachael would think back to when they first met, now two years ago and wondered how their relationship came to this. There was his obsession with timekeeping but apart from that he was good to her then. He took her out to expensive restaurants and showered her with gifts. He made her feel like the most important person in the whole world which was something she had not experienced at that point for a long time.

At times like these, when she felt so depleted, there was one thing that kept her going and that was reminding herself that he saved her life. She was grateful to him for that.

Rachael was one of those unfortunate girls who seemed to fall in love with the wrong type of guy. Each relationship ended up in violence. At the tender age of seventeen, her first boyfriend was Jack. He repeatedly told her that she was ugly, stupid and a waste of space. When Jack brought her to tears, he felt completely satisfied and then carried on by pretending to sulk as if it was all her fault that he was being so nasty. She would wipe away the tears and beg for forgiveness until he put his arms around her. She did not know why she stayed with him but she just could not bear the thought of not having him in her life. However, after five years of suffering mental abuse, Rachael finally left him after he slapped her.

Sadly, two years later, her next relationship was with Aiden and all too quickly it followed the same path and it did not take long to break her spirit. She accepted the occasional slap in the face until before long the beatings grew more and more frequent and aggressive. Rachael now believed that she deserved everything that she got because somehow it was her fault. To avoid visible bruises, Aiden would repeatedly punch her in the stomach. Rachael would only whimper and curl up into a ball. It took four years before he got bored of her and left.

Tragically, just a few days after Aiden left, she fell into the hands of yet another bad boy called Bradley. Rachael felt herself spinning in a vicious circle, unable to stop the rotations that muddied her mind. Just a few weeks into this relationship, she discovered that he could not control his anger and would suddenly burst into a terrible rage. She did everything possible to prevent his fury but of course, this was not always possible. Six years later, after suffering much abuse, she was worn out. What remained was a shell, vacant and numb with no personality whatsoever. One evening, Bradley came home from work, obviously agitated by something. Sensing the danger, Rachael tried to slip away quietly into the shadows of the bedroom and wait until his mood improved. She slid down the wall in the corner of the room and folded her arms around her legs. The silence was deadly, like the calm before the storm. Without any warning, he threw the door open and grabbed her tightly by the arm and pulled her up until she stood on her feet. Rachael winced but remained quiet.

'Get your shoes on. I want to go for a walk.' He growled with his face almost touching Rachael's, spraying spittle evenly across hers. He let go of her and stormed out of the room.

Rachael quickly obeyed and by the time she got to the front door, he had already walked half way down the street. She ran swiftly to catch up with him. Before long they reached an alleyway but she did not want to follow him into it. She had a sense of dread and knew what could be waiting for her in its darkness. Even though she was weak and broken, there still remained in her the desire to live. She tensed up as the alleyway could only mean one thing. It was dark and rarely used. It was the perfect place for Bradley to take his anger out on her. Rachael began to shake and tears formed in her eyes. For the first time in a long while, she felt truly frightened. She froze to the spot, shivering.

'Get here!' Bradley bellowed fiercely. The darkness of the night blackened his cold eyes and the moon that shone behind him made him into a spooky shadow, creating the image of Satan himself.

Rachael could not move. She wanted to run away but was so petrified that her legs refused to budge.

Bradley grabbed her arm and dragged her further into the alleyway. When they were deep enough into it, he swung around and punched her in the face. Blood gushed out of her nose and the pain exploded. The next blow was to the base of her spine causing her to collapse on the floor. He began to scream obscenities at her as he repeatedly kicked and kicked and kicked. His foot landed in her ribs; her face; her head. With each blow, that little hope to live faded away and the light behind her eyes flickered and switched off. Rachael silently welcomed death to take her away from the hell that she was in.

Suddenly, the beating stopped and she sighed with relief, thinking her life was over.

Rachael felt warm, gentle arms wrap around her body that lifted her up so easily as if she was a feather. Her broken body flopped into those strong arms like a rag doll. Her final thought was that her guardian angel had finally come for her and then she fainted.

Danny, had indeed, saved her life.

After laying unconscious for five days in hospital, Rachael finally woke up. The nurses told her how a brave and handsome hero walked into the hospital, carrying her in his arms. He was covered in her blood and she looked such a pitiful sight that for a few moments they mistook her for being dead. Once he delivered her to safety, he simply disappeared.

It was a few weeks later, when Rachael was feeling much stronger and able to go home that one of the nurses entered her room giggling excitedly, informing her that the hero had returned to visit her. As he entered, the nurse made a quick exit, still giggling like a silly schoolgirl. Rachael's eyes settled on the man who she was indebted to. He was nothing like how she imagined. In front of her was an attractive but not devilishly handsome man as the nurses described. He was just below average height and stocky, making his physique look strangely rectangular. His hands were in his pockets and his shoulders were hunched up, almost reaching his ears. It gave him the appearance of not having a neck. His head cocked to the left and she had a strange sensation that he was viewing her sideways.

Her eyes widened in disbelief when she realised who he was. There could only be one person in the whole world who looked like that and that was Danny, the weird little boy who sat at the back of her tutor group at school so many years ago. This was her hero, the man who showed up just in the nick of time to save her from the jaws of death.

'Danny,' she whispered and found herself getting slightly breathless.

He gave her a shy grin but remained silent. He took a couple of small steps towards her. In the past, she would have found his motion revolting as it reminded her of a slug sliding across the path after a spell of torrential rain. The distinct smell of damp after the rain, wafted up her nose. Rachael had always associated that particular stench with slugs and therefore, Danny. However, as he approached her, the smell no longer seemed so offensive. Again, he slid across the floor towards her, grinning animatedly. Rachael felt a shiver run up her spine. Again, very surprisingly, the shiver was not one of disgust but one of a desperate yearning to be touched.

She studied him once more and found that his body did not look like a block of wood anymore but muscular and strong. His sideways glance was more sweet and bashful. She noted how his black hair settled in tight curls on his masculine face. Those blue eyes were intense and appeared to savour her lustfully which made her tremble with delight. He was her hero but soon, he would be her man and this excited Rachael immensely.

Now here she was, taking a burnt lasagne out of the oven, concerned that Danny would suspect that her timing was wrong. Leaving the dish on the side, she ran to open the window and frantically fanned the air to get rid of the smell. After a moment, she returned back to the lasagne and realised that it was only the béchamel sauce that was ruined on top. Carefully, she scraped the hard, blackened layer off and replaced it with some of the sauce that she kept back in a pot, just in case. She had learnt from experience to be prepared for any eventuality. Returning the dish to the oven, she sighed with relief. Dinner would be on time.

Danny was as regimental as ever, she thought to herself upon hearing the key rattle in the door. She began to visualise what he would do step by step. This was easy, as his movements around the house were just as predictable as his timings. At this moment, he would be stepping into the house. He would take his coat off and drop it onto the floor where it would stay until she picked it up and hung it on the peg, ready for the next day. He was just taking his shoes off and putting on the slippers that she had placed by the door for him.

Before going upstairs to freshen up, he would now be peeking into the dining room to check that the table had been laid, ready for his dinner. Satisfied, he would now march up the stairs and come down at exactly six-thirty when he would sit at the table with his plate before him. Rachael could hear his soft footfalls until he reached the bathroom door.

It was six-thirty and Rachael heard his steps as he sprinted down the stairs. As Danny settled into his seat and lifted his knife and fork, Rachael stood by the side of him waiting for him to speak. Danny looked intently down at the lasagne and Rachael was sure that he was trying very hard to find a fault. Suddenly, his nose twitched and his expression curdled.

'Did something burn? I can smell it!' He stared at Rachael, assessing her every move.

'No, of course not.' Rachael tried to be convincing but her eyes widened and she began fiddling nervously with her hands. Danny's eyes dropped towards them and he knew that she was hiding something from him. She continued, 'Look, you can see that the lasagne is perfect. Perhaps the oven needs cleaning again. You know how food gets trapped in there. I will do that tomorrow... Yes the first task I will set myself is to clean the oven.' She was babbling and consciously willed herself to stop. She winced at the ridiculous things that were coming out of her stupid mouth. She hated cleaning the oven but Danny insisted that she had to do it twice a week.

Danny kept his eyes on Rachael as he chewed on a piece of lasagne. A slither of melted cheese bopped on his chin then dropped back onto the plate. Rachael watched this with neither humour nor repugnance.

Picking up his glass, which had been filled with a crisp, perfectly chilled white wine, placed it into his mouth and washed the food down in one almighty gulp. He still kept his eyes on her.

'Tomorrow?' he suddenly questioned, 'I would rather you did it after you washed the dishes. If a job needs doing...' He motioned with his hands the rest of the saying. It was one that Rachael knew all too well. 'It is only six-thirty five. It is still early.'

Rachael hesitated, startled by the suggestion. After washing the dishes, she had to mop the floor. Besides, she had planned to take a long soak in the bath as Danny would be watching football from seven o'clock. He never wanted to be disturbed at those times. She had been looking forward to having some solitude and rest.

'The football is on tonight and I thought I could take a bath.' She tried to reason with him but was annoyed by how squeaky and pathetic her voice sounded.

Danny's glare intensified and for a moment he remained silent. He returned his attention to the plate before him and dug his fork sharply into the lasagne so that it grated along the plate, leaving a scratch. Taking a large mouthful, he smiled contentedly. He chewed for a very long time and then swallowed dramatically. Cocking his head to the left, he grinned as he stared at her sideways, 'This is perfect, and the best food you have cooked so far.'

Rachael remained still but she could feel the relief wash over every inch of her body.

'Take your bath, you deserve it.'

Danny's comment hung in the air and Rachael was stunned by it. She had not seen that sideways grin for a long time and missed it greatly. She almost skipped back into the kitchen, bewildered yet overjoyed by the sudden compliment. In a much more cheerful mood, she began to pile up the pots and pans in the sink. She began to let her thoughts run wild inside her mind, 'Danny had his ways but he was not a bad man. He may have never said 'I love you' but he does have feelings for me. Anyway, I have enough love for the both of us.'

'Don't forget that we are going away for the reunion thing,' Danny called out to her from the dining room.

Rachael barely heard a word of what he was saying so left the dishes and returned to the room where he was sitting. She noted that he had finished every bit of his meal and was completely satisfied. He had pushed the chair back from the table as though he needed to create space for his full stomach.

'Sorry, what was that?' she asked timidly.

'The weekend away in a few weeks time. You must start airing the suitcases.' Danny was clearly in a good mood. His eyes glistened with excitement. 'Imagine their faces when they see we are a couple, eh?' He chuckled cheekily.

It warmed her heart to think he was so proud to show the others that she was his partner. She also felt the same as he did by this prospect. Rachael knew that women found him appealing and tried to flirt with him, especially when they realised what he did for a living. Other women's advances on Danny never worried her because she knew that he would never respond to them and would always return home to her. Seeing that this reunion had made him so happy, Rachael began to think that it was a blessing in disguise.

'Off you pop, the dishes will not do themselves,' Danny chirped and Rachael was sure that she could see that same intense, lustful stare that he had given her all those years ago at the hospital. Quickly taking away his plate and glass, she pranced back into the kitchen.

While in the kitchen her thoughts returned back to the reunion. It could bring them closer together and… dare she hope… might make him consider marriage. With this thought floating around in her mind she began to wash the dishes. She hummed to herself and decided that she could probably clean the oven before she had a bath.

CHAPTER SIX

Barry stood in the middle of the lounge and inspected the finished result. He had been extremely busy in the last few weeks, devoting all his time and energy into the house by working all day and well into the night to make sure that everything would be ready in time for when his guests arrived. His appearance suffered and he began to look like a caveman. His unwashed hair was matted with paint and he grew a thick and bushy beard. For the first time in years, he neglected the gym sessions but due to the physical effort that was required for the job, his body remained toned. He barely ate or drank but when he did, it was nutritious and provided the slow burning calories essential to sustain him.

He surveyed the room carefully, searching for any imperfections and when there was none to be found, he smiled gleefully. He was proud of what he had achieved and hoped that his aunt would have been equally impressed by his efforts. He always loved the homely and welcoming feel to the house but disliked the old fashioned furniture and fittings. His aunt was an amazing person but her tastes were antiquated. When he was a young boy it never bothered him but it did now. His aim was to keep it informal and simple but updated with a more modern style.

Gone were the dark green, velvet curtains and the floral three piece suite. The hideous multicoloured carpet was also removed and to Barry's surprise, there was a beautiful oak wooden floor hidden underneath it that begged to be displayed in all its glory. It was a sin that such expensive flooring had been hidden for so many years. It was about time someone gave it the care and attention that it deserved. Carefully, and with some trepidation, he had sanded the wood down and varnished it. Light, cream curtains now framed the windows which were cleaned until they were crystal clear. A light green leather settee and matching arm chairs were placed facing each other, adjacent to the fireplace. It would be a nice cosy place for the guests to socialise.

Even though Barry made significant changes inside and outside of the property, it was never his intention to remove all the essence of his dear aunt. He kept some of the attractive cupboards and ornaments that she treasured. The most difficult project for him to tackle was his aunt's bedroom. This was once her intimate space and sadly the place where she died. It was where Barry spent a lot of his time while caring for her. When she could no longer manage to hold a book, he would read to her as she relaxed or fell asleep in the middle of a story or poem. Most of the time they spent talking about the happy times they shared together and her hopes for his future that she would never be a part of.

Sadness filled the room and yet he knew that he whole heartedly tried to make each day count. Barry left this room to last. He decided to make the least changes here by simply giving it a coat of paint and replacing the bed and linen in the hope that she would have approved of the alterations that he made. Once the paint dried, he would put back all of her photographs, paintings and ornaments where they belonged. Barry decided to claim the room for himself. He could not bear the thought of anyone else staying there and felt that she would have liked it if he made it his own.

In three days time his guests would arrive and he felt a strange mixture of excitement and nervousness about it. To his surprise, he no longer cared about showing off how much he had changed from being the joke of the classroom to a very handsome man. He was more concerned about the outcome of their reunion. Would they all get on after all these years? They all must have changed and it would be interesting to know what they had all become. It would be nice to see them again and perhaps if the weekend was a success they could keep in touch and remain friends. How wonderful that would be, making a fresh start and burying all the demons forever. Soon, he would find out if he did the right thing in sending out the invitations. Barry smirked and shook his head thinking how he had mellowed with age. It was all down to his aunt and the happy environment that she provided for him. Things could have been very different if he had been taken into care after his mother died. It was futile to dwell on these things as shortly all would be revealed but for now there was still so much to organize. There was still the shopping to do and to give some consideration as to what they could do for the whole weekend. He wanted it to be a memorable occasion, one that they would never forget. When they first arrive, he would have to give them time to settle into their rooms and then have dinner. Their first meal would have to be something that he cooked himself and not something out of a packet. It would show them that he made the effort of giving them a warm welcome into his home. He paused and once again, chuckled and shook his head. It had been a long time since he had thought of this place as being his home but now it felt different somehow, maybe because he owned it. He never imagined that he would warm to the idea so much.

Barry decided that Saturday morning, after breakfast, he would show them around the area. There were so many lovely places to visit and if they felt more energetic there were beautiful walks that they could go on. It would be nice to do something as a group. Perhaps they could have lunch in one of the restaurants before setting back to the house for a rest. At this point, Barry took a notepad from the table and ripped the first page out. Taking a pen out of his shirt pocket, he sat down by the table and started to scribble down his ideas. After a rest, it would be good to give everyone time to do whatever they wanted to. They would be free to carry on socialising or spending the time alone in their room for a while if they preferred. They would all meet up for another home cooked dinner which would be served at seven o'clock. After they finished eating, Barry wanted the evening to continue in the lounge and if they wished, play party games.

Sighing, Barry put his pen down on the table. He read through what he had written so far. He began to realise how much effort and money would have to be put into this venture. They could pay for the food in the restaurant themselves but everything else would be his responsibility. He had never entertained anyone before and although he had been present at many parties, he had not spared a thought as to what actually went into the planning of such things. He had only been concerned about dodging the drunken tarts and getting paid at the end of the night.

Returning to his piece of paper, he picked up his pen again. He imagined that on Sunday after breakfast everyone would want to pack their suitcases, ready for the journey home. It would be prudent to be prepared in case they wanted lunch before leaving. 'More expense,' he mumbled to himself.

Barry scratched his beard, which had started to itch and annoy him. He had always preferred to be clean shaven. He was so obsessed with the house that his appearance was the last thing on his mind; well almost. The first thing that he would do now is to have a shower and shave before going out to the shops to get all the necessary groceries and beverages. Even though it would prove to be expensive, he could not wait for the weekend to start. He hoped that it would be full of laughs and great surprises.

CHAPTER SEVEN

Jim sat in his car, watching the raindrops slither down his windscreen, making the house that he was parked in front of, look blurry. As the rain got heavier, the house contorted, giving the impression that it was alive and engaged in a menacing, tribal dance. He had been sitting there waiting for ten minutes now and began tapping the steering wheel impatiently.

He had no idea why he was getting so agitated when he knew from experience that Sarah was never on time. At long last, he could see her stumbling down the garden path, weighed down with three bags. She grimaced, indicating to Jim how heavy her luggage was, as she was dragging them slowly towards the boot of the car. Due to the lack of sympathy, he had no intention of getting out of the car to help her. They were just going for two nights and by the look of it, she had packed enough items to last a month. He simply pressed a button that opened the boot and listened as she dumped everything in. After slamming it shut, she opened the passenger door and sat down, looking absolutely drenched. Just as Jim turned towards her to say something, she opened the door and jumped out. As she ran back up the path, she twirled round and shouted, 'I forgot my make-up kit. I won't be two minutes.'

That was fifteen minutes ago and Jim was still waiting.

Jim was feeling frustrated by this point as he had no idea why it should take so long to fetch a vanity case. Sarah knew perfectly well that he wanted them to be on their way by four o'clock to avoid the traffic. Even though the rain was pelting down, he was itching to get out of the car and fetch her. The only thing that was stopping him from doing this was the fact that she still lived at home with her parents and her sister, Katie. It would be difficult to barge in and demand that they should leave immediately. He knew the family since childhood and had no wish to show any aggression in front of them. They were always kind and happy to have him as their daughter's friend.

Jim was an only child and always wished he had a brother or sister and because Katie was much younger than him, he adopted her for the role as a niece. When Katie was a little girl, she had a dry sense of humour and was witty beyond her years. Some of the things that she came out with made him laugh so much that his stomach ached. She had been an energetic and intelligent girl and he adored her.

When Katie reached the age of twenty four, the relationship between them changed. Jim felt awkward to be around her. She acted as though she had a crush on him. Every time she saw him she would blow him kisses and cuddle him all too intimately. He was convinced that Katie enjoyed watching him squirm and her behaviour succeeded in making him feel extremely uncomfortable. When she got too close, he would gently push her away and when she deliberately bent over in a short skirt, he made it obvious that he was looking the other way. She knew that he was gay but this did not dissuade her in any way but simply intensified her bad conduct as if it was some kind of a game that she took as a challenge to end up victorious. It made him feel quite sad because like an uncle, he wanted to take care of her and he would have done anything to make her happy. Now, all that was all ruined and it would never be the same again.

For some unknown reason, Katie's parents appeared unaware of their youngest daughter's antics and he was reluctant to point it out in fear of upsetting them. They had always played a big part in his life and supported him with everything. Therefore, he felt that it would be best to say nothing in the hope that Katie would get bored and leave him alone.

Jim could not think when he actually realised that he preferred men to girls but he clearly remembered his first relationship. He and Archie had been friends since the start of year seven in Secondary school. They hung around together and shared everything from football magazines to their packed lunches. Archie had an incredibly sweet tooth while Jim preferred savoury snacks. When it came to lunchtime, they would swap some of the food that their mothers packed for them. Archie took the chocolate bar and biscuits and Jim had the crisps and peanuts. Sarah was always with them and often mocked that they were more like a married couple. They too would laugh but wondered if in some way, there was an element of truth in what she said. Soon, Sarah spent her breaks and lunch times with her female friends, talking about boys and giving make-up tips. Archie and Jim's relationship grew stronger until one day, when they were both sixteen, they admitted their true feelings for each other and secretly became a couple. Neither wanted to let anyone else know their secret apart from Sarah.

A year later, Jim decided to tell his parents. The prospect filled him with dread as they were a traditional, middle class family with firmly imbedded values that were proudly passed from generation to generation. During many sleepless nights, Jim ran through various ways in which to tell them. Each method began with him asking his parents to sit down as he had something important to tell them. However, it did not happen as he planned. All was revealed on his seventeenth birthday celebration, at a local restaurant, with his Auntie Jean, Uncle Brian and their spoilt daughter Bethany in attendance. His Uncle was not just an intolerant man but a blatantly rude one as well. He was known for hollering out racist and chauvinistic remarks, leaving his wife looking incredibly embarrassed. This time, he decided to make homophobic remarks; just for a change.

'They get everything they deserve those poofs.'

Jim felt himself tense up.

'Bloody dirty poofters deserve a kicking.'

Jim clenched his hands into fists under the table. His lips formed a straight line as he pressed them together tightly.

'That's where all the diseases started from... poofs.'

Blood pumped fiercely inside Jim's chest and shot up to his head making it pound. His face turned a deep shade of crimson.

His uncle was just about to say something else but only had time to open his smug mouth when Jim shot out of his chair and shouted deliriously, 'I'm gay! Do I deserve a beating too?'

The whole room went quiet and everyone stared at him. He looked at his mother who sat as still as a statue, mouth wide open. He could see the disappointment in her eyes. His father was worse. He shrank back into his chair with a look of total disgust. Bethany was the first to speak. She giggled and screamed with delight, 'Now this is funny.' She clapped her hands together in a mock applause.

Again, he returned his attention to his parents. His mother had remained completely motionless and his father averted his eyes away from his son as though unable to look at him.

Almost in a whisper, Jim whined, 'Mum? Dad?' His parents said nothing.

Pushing the chair away, Jim stormed out of the restaurant but before managing to open the door he could hear his uncle mumble, 'I always knew there was something wrong with that boy.'

His parents remained silent.

He could never forget that time when he ran to Sarah's house, crying. It was raining just as heavily as it was now. Deeply hurt by the reaction he received from his parents, Jim burst into tears and stumbled through the torrential rain. He did not have a specific destination in mind but found himself standing outside Sarah's house. He pressed the bell once and within seconds

Sarah's mother opened the door. She gazed at Jim, who was standing at the door soaking wet and shivering. His eyes were red and the tears were still running down his cheeks. She gasped and held her hands in front of her mouth then opened her arms wide to receive him. Once inside the warm house, Jim dropped to his knees and Sarah's mother crouched down to put her arms around him. They remained that way for some time until Jim had no more tears left to shed.

He told her what had happened in the restaurant and Sarah's mother listened sympathetically. Once he finished what he was telling her, she said, 'Oh Jim, I know your parents well enough to know that they love you very much, unconditionally. Being a parent is not as easy as you think. You want the best for your child. Yes, I know you are seventeen but you will always be their child.'

Jim found her soothing, gentle voice calming and listened without saying a word.

'It must have been a shock for them that's all. You certainly chose your moment I must say. Not like hitting them with it. A private conversation would have been more appropriate.' She sighed heavily, cradling Jim in her arms. 'What's done is done and now they know. Now, give them the time to take it all in. They just worry about you, that's all. Every parent's dream is for their son or daughter to settle down, get married, have a family. It's just how it is. They simply need the time to get used it.'

Jim turned his face up towards hers and asked, 'Will they accept me?'

'Without a doubt, they already have. They just don't know it right now as they are stunned by your revelation.'

Sitting in the car, watching the rain make patterns across his windshield, Jim smiled to himself. Sarah's mother was right. That night he returned home to find the door was already wide open and his mother was standing in the doorway, waiting for him. She squeezed him tightly and together they cried. His dad patted him on the back but could not find the right words to express himself. Nothing was needed to be said as their actions said it all. Yes, they did accept him and more importantly, they loved him unconditionally as Sarah's mother told him.

Sarah suddenly pulled the passenger door open and practically fell into the car. Jim jumped at that moment as he had been deep in thought.

'Told you I wouldn't be long,' she chirped.

'You were more than fifteen minutes,' Jim whined.

'I couldn't find it at first. Things are never where you expect them to be.' Sarah rolled her eyes comically.

'You couldn't find it for two reasons, one – your room is a tip. Two – you never wear make-up. You stopped by the time you got to twenty,' Jim commented sharply.

Sarah huffed. 'That's not true. I just make sure that when I put it on my face, the effect is more natural.'

Jim studied her face intensely as he switched the engine back on. Sarah closed her eyes firmly, pushed her chin out towards him and pouted. When she opened them again, she fluttered her eyelashes. Jim smirked and chuckled, 'You couldn't be sexy no matter how hard you try. By the way, I still cannot see any make-up at all.'

Sarah huffed once more and then smiled, 'You wouldn't understand the meaning of a sexy woman anyway.'

The rain was lashing down so hard that Jim had to put the windscreen wipers on full speed. He knew that the harsh weather condition would undoubtedly slow down their journey. As they headed out towards the motorway, both seemed lost in their own thoughts. Both were thinking about the weekend ahead. Sarah was still unsure whether going was such a good idea and the severe torrential rain seemed like a warning that they should stop the car and return home. Trying to calm herself down she tried to convince herself that she was being silly and unreasonable. She sighed and looked through the window at the grey sky above and decided that if it began to thunder then that would definitely be a bad omen insisting that they should not have gone.

Jim appeared to be fully concentrating on the road but he wondered what the others would think of him now. At school, many suspected that he did not like girls and many jokes were made on account of this. Of course, he laughed them off, even though inside he felt threatened, confused and very vulnerable. After leaving at sixteen, both he and Archie had lost contact with the rest of the tutor group and in fact, with anyone they knew from school. At times he would think about this and find it odd that most of them still lived in the same town but he had never bumped into any of them. They say that it is a small world and yet he felt that his town was such a huge place as you could easily be lost amongst the throngs of people that walked past you every day.

Breaking the silence, Jim turned the radio on. At once, the cheerful DJ announced, 'Well folks, it's pretty dreary out there at the moment and it will soon get worse. Thunder is predicted across all areas with winds of up to sixty miles an hour. If you are on the road, please take care and if there is no need to travel... don't.'

Sarah stared wide-eyed at the radio but remained quiet.

'Typical, that's all we need, eh?' Jim commented, 'Let's just hope we don't hit any floods.'

Just as he said this, first came lightening and then thunder burst from the dark sky into a loud roar.

CHAPTER EIGHT

Emma gazed out of the taxi window and as they drove along the motorway, she could feel the car struggle against the wind which had strengthened since she left her flat. The car was rocking precariously from side to side, making her feel slightly nauseous. She could hear the driver mutter profanities from under his breath and silently smiled to herself. For some reason listening to the taxi driver moaning, humoured her. It seemed as if they all hated their job. Since moving away from home, she had taken quite a few taxi rides, especially on long journeys. It was a luxury that she could barely afford but essential to enable her from getting from one place to another without any problem. Emma found buses difficult because inconsiderate women with pushchairs and prams often took the space allocated for disabled passengers, leaving no room for her and the wheelchair and as a result forcing her to wait for the next bus. Emma also found it difficult to travel by train. She was sick to death of ringing for assistance twenty-four hours before travelling, only to find out that the particular station she needed was not step free or that there was not enough staff to provide the assistance she required. Then there was the matter of having to change trains; it was all very exhausting and frustrating. Truthfully, if she ever dared to admit, it was very embarrassing to be so reliant on strangers in order to do the simple things that everyone else took for granted. The taxi, although expensive, was a better option for her personally.

Thunder growled angrily from above in the same way as the driver continued to curse in the front seat. He was starting to make her feel rather uncomfortable as his whining increased in volume. Emma decided to turn her attention to what was going on outside and was sure that she had never seen so much rain fall in such a short space of time. The road ahead looked like a river and the car made tidal waves as it continued its journey. Although they had only been driving for two hours, it felt like many more.

The driver cautiously slowed down to take the bends in the road. The lanes became narrower with only a few houses dotted around. There was a huge difference between a city and the countryside. The scenery here was picturesque with impressive, green hills and an array of trees and flowers lining the rural roads. Nevertheless, Emma found it all very unsettling. Its emptiness was eerie. The sun was smothered behind dirty, grey clouds that were dragged across the sky by the strong winds like ghostly servants. There was a continuous smog that prevented any rays of sunshine to poke through. There were no signs of life; not even one person could be seen dashing home to shelter from the rain; no birds nestling between the branches of the trees and no animals roaming around looking for food.

The driver suddenly stopped the car without warning, causing Emma to lunge forward with such force that she could hear her neck click. He then said abruptly, 'We are here love.'

Leaning forward, she could just about see the house at the end of the driveway. It looked so magnificent that it made Emma gasp in surprise. The gates were open, allowing the driver to drop her off at the front door. Emma noticed that there was only one car on the driveway which obviously belonged to Barry. She was the first guest to arrive and this made her feel nervous. Since her accident, she preferred to remain in the background at functions but this meant that she would be the centre of attention with no one there to take the pressure off her.

'That will be exactly fifty-eight pounds darling,' said the driver as he twisted round in his seat. Even though he used terms of endearment, the tone of his voice was flat and unfriendly. His face was as gloomy as the weather outside and his pale blue eyes were without any emotion. Saggy, old skin dangled over a mouth that turned downwards on its corners and his scrawny neck was wrinkled by the strain of having to face her.

Emma quickly turned her attention to her purse that she speedily took out from her handbag. She started to count the notes out and stopped. She then asked him politely, 'Could you be so kind as to place my wheelchair by the door for me?'

The driver groaned and melodramatically rolled his eyes. He put his flat cap on his head and once more cursed before exiting the car. While he took the wheelchair out of the boot, Emma finished counting the money, taking an extra five pounds for a tip.

The driver, without bothering to unfold the wheelchair, placed it close to her side of the car. It crashed to the ground and instead of picking it up, he dashed back to his seat with great dexterity, swept his cap off and shook it over the vacant seat beside him. Emma was stunned by all this.

Once settled, the driver turned around, pushing a spindly, liver spotted hand through the gap between the two front seats, ready to receive his payment. Seeing Emma's shocked expression, he shouted, 'Bloody hell woman, you don't expect me to help you to get into the damn thing in this rain?' Nodding his head towards the wheelchair outside.

Emma had never been so ill treated or spoken to with such vehemence by a taxi driver before. It shook her up and left her speechless. She removed the five pound tip from the pile of notes in her hand and shoved the correct amount into his hand.

Finally, finding her voice, Emma replied with a firm tone, 'I can manage myself thank you.' She swung the door open and felt her arm being pulled as a gust of wind pushed it with great force. The rain pelted icily on her head and she tried not to shiver as it trickled down her neck and back. She reached for the chair, which was difficult, as it lay a foot away from the car. Barely reaching down, she stretched as far as possible and hooked three fingers through one of the wheels and dragged it closer. She slowly opened it up. Emma had to do this by herself every day and it was never such a problem as it was now. With the wind and rain pushing against her and the nonchalant stare of the driver; her movements were clumsy as she tried to get out of the car. Finally, she was able to swing her legs out and hoist herself up and into the chair. Reaching back into the taxi, she pulled her handbag out from the seat and planted it down onto her legs. Drenched, she lifted her head indignantly and slammed the door shut. She had barely moved away from the car, when the driver reversed and sped off.

'Good riddance to you,' she growled and turned towards the house. She sighed with relief to see that Barry had fixed a ramp by the side of the stairs. Taking a deep breath and mustering all the courage that she could, she wheeled herself up to the front door and rang the bell.

Almost immediately, the door opened and Emma looked up in wonder at the man who was standing before her. At first, she thought that it could not possibly be Barry, the fat sweaty kid from her tutor group. This man was very fit, in both senses of the word. He had a gorgeous smile and the way he leaned against the door frame suggested self-confidence and perhaps a little hint of flirtatiousness. She felt her cheeks redden and quickly looked away from his face. He was staring at her intently and leaned closer towards her.

'Emma? I guess it's you.' Barry began the conversation. His voice was cheerful and welcoming.

Emma's whole head felt hot with embarrassment. She glanced back up at him and started to recognise aspects of the young Barry that she used to know. His hair was still wavy and dark. The eyes were as she remembered, clear, azure blue and beautiful to look at.

'Well, I guess I must be the only person turning up in a wheelchair.' As she spoke those words she felt silly for saying them. She gave a sheepish smile and felt ridiculous for it. The taxi driver with his attitude and calling her chair, 'that thing' left her feeling deeply upset and inadequate and she just could not shrug it off.

Barry's smile broadened, 'No, I mean you haven't changed much. You look incredible and so young. You must have lived a good life.' Now, it was Barry's turn to feel foolish. How could he even suggest that she could possibly have had a good life? He could not imagine what she must have gone through since the accident. He looked down at her and realised that she was still out in the rain. 'Oh my goodness, how terrible of me. You must be freezing. Come in, come in. I'll show you to your room so that you can sort yourself out and get out of those wet clothes. I have put the bed in the study so that you do not need to go upstairs. Luckily, this house does have a downstairs bathroom that you can use.'

'That is very thoughtful of you,' Emma replied.

When they reached the study, Barry opened the door to let Emma in. He then smiled and said, 'If there is anything else that you might need, please let me know. Oh yes, I almost forgot; here is the key to your door. Make yourself comfortable and I will see you later, whenever you are ready that is. You will find me just down the corridor in the kitchen.'

Once Emma was alone, she put her handbag down and looked around the room. She was sure that there was the smell of fresh paint, not only in her room but out in the corridor as well. Barry must have just decorated the house, she thought to herself. The bed looked comfortable and inviting with a blue duvet cover and matching pillow cases. She wheeled herself to the mirror that was placed on a small dressing table.

It was just the right height for her and guessed that it was obviously another thoughtful idea of Barry's.

She studied her own reflection in the mirror. Even though she had been in the rain for quite some time, she still looked quite possible. Her make-up had not been washed off or smudged by the rain and her hair was beginning to dry. She then decided to go back to where she left her handbag to get the hairbrush. After rummaging around for a little while, she found it and moved again towards the dresser. Once more, she looked at herself in the mirror when suddenly something caught the corner of her eyes. She looked at the reflection of the window in the mirror to find two pale blue eyes staring at her. She screeched and dropped her hairbrush. Someone was watching her. She turned around slowly so that she could see more clearly who it could be and as she did this, felt her whole body becoming numb with fear. The weird taxi driver was glaring at her. His lips were curled up menacingly and he began to tap on the window. His flapping skin swayed back and forth over his jaw bone as he was trying to say something to her. Emma could not hear him but by the look on his face, it could not have been anything pleasant. She quickly wheeled herself to the window and drew the curtains shut. She moved away and stopped in the middle of the room. Panting and feeling petrified, she remained motionless. Her fingers curled around the wheels of the chair, making her knuckles white. Her arm muscles ached but still she clung tightly. Thoughts rushed around in her head deliriously, 'What does he want? Did he just curse me? Has he gone yet?' She wanted to call Barry but was unsure of what to do. Did he not hear her scream?

Someone banged on the front door. Boom – boom – boom. Someone was definitely determined to get in. It was him, he wanted to get her. She began to whine in a desperate whisper, 'Don't open the door... please.'

Just at that moment she could hear Barry walking towards the front door shouting, 'OK, OK I'm coming.' Emma could not hear anything else until the front door slammed shut. Steps thudded on the floor, getting closer and closer to her room. Emma felt her heartbeat quicken its pace. She held her breath, trying to be as quiet as possible. She was now pleading, 'Go away... please... just go away.'

The door opened and Emma screamed as loudly as she possibly could.

Barry instantly held his hands to his head and winced. A familiar bag dangled from one of his hands. 'Jeez, Emma what in the hell is wrong with you.' He noticed that the room was dark and the curtains were drawn. Words failed him and he just stared in bewilderment at his guest.

Emma sighed and placed her head in her hands, 'I'm sorry. I don't know what has got into me.' Her face was pale and her body was trembling.

'It was just your taxi driver. He noticed that you had left your bag on the back seat and drove back to give it to you. The driver was not happy because he had already travelled a fair distance before he spotted it. He even charged me twenty pounds for his trouble, can you believe that?' Barry explained.

Emma looked at the bag that he was holding and sighed once more. 'I totally forgot about it. I was in such a fluster because he was so rude to me.'

'And a bit creepy if you ask me,' Barry agreed. 'Well, he won't come back again. I hope not anyway. I am not paying another twenty quid.'

'What a start to the weekend. You must think I'm a complete and utter idiot.' Emma managed to say this with a smile.

'Nah, it's probably just the weather. It is rather nasty out there,' Barry replied whilst looking out of the window. 'Look, when you have finished sorting yourself out, come to the kitchen and I will crack open a bottle of wine. I don't know what time anyone else will arrive but we might as well get the party started.'

'Sounds like a good idea.' Emma brightened up. She was rather annoyed with herself for being so jumpy and irrational. She hoped that the wine would settle her nerves.

CHAPTER NINE

Emma made her way to the kitchen. She could hear Barry opening and closing cupboard doors and the tinkling of glasses. Suddenly, the distinct sound of a champagne cork popped and there was the clatter of a bottle being shoved into a bucket full of ice. It was obvious that he took pride in looking after his guests and she found this extremely endearing. She stopped by the kitchen door and watched him as he placed plates full of savoury bites on the table. His face was full of concentration and as he frowned, he pursed his lips causing dimples to form on both sides of his cheeks. Emma noticed that his big muscles were visible beneath his shirt and his jeans fit snugly over his thick, athletic legs. She could not believe how much he had changed. It was obvious that he was obsessed with keeping fit and she wondered what could have caused such a dramatic change in his personality. She knew that he had been constantly bullied for the most part of his school life and yet he did not appear embittered by that. On the contrary, it seemed that he turned out to be a strong, pleasant, confident man and one that has done very well financially for himself considering the size of his house.

Once again, she found the situation more than a little bizarre. Here she was, staying in a stranger's house. Apart from being in the same class at school with Barry, she knew very little about him. He was just one of those unpopular kids at the back of the classroom who once broke a chair by sitting on it. She barely acknowledged him when they were in the same room or passed each other in the corridor. They were never friends, they simply remained a sea of faces that one met but never got to know.

Barry caught sight of Emma and gave her a warm smile. 'I thought champagne was an appropriate way to welcome my first and only guest so far. Hopefully, the others will also turn up soon. There is a little bit of food, nothing much, just something light to keep everyone going until dinner at about 9ish, giving everyone time to settle in.'

Emma entered the room and scanned the plates on the table. There were various salads and meats as well as pastries and a fruit platter. 'A bit of food? This is lovely. Shouldn't we have waited for the others before opening the champagne?'

'Don't worry, I do have more bottles in the fridge.' Barry grinned shyly and handed a full glass of champagne to her which she accepted gratefully. She took a sip and nodded at Barry to indicate that it tasted divine.

Barry raised his glass towards Emma and said, 'Cheers and may this be the best reunion in the whole world.'

'I second that,' Emma agreed, taking another, more generous sip from her glass. 'So, what do you do for a living? It must be a good job if you can afford all this.' She waved her glass in the air while looking around the room.

Barry put his head down and gave a nervous laugh. 'Actually, I have a flat in London which is small but adequate. This was my aunt's house. She left it to me in her will.'

'Oh I'm so sorry,' Emma replied.

'It's ok. It was a long time ago. This is the first time that I am actually using this house.' Barry tried hard to hide his feelings but his eyes revealed that he was still feeling the pain by the loss of his aunt.

Emma, at this point wanted to change the subject to something more pleasant and show her interest in him. 'How is your mum? I remember she came to the school play.'

'Yeah, the one where I played Humpty Dumpty and was pushed off the wall,' Barry replied with bitterness in his voice.

'Oh God, I remember that. I wasn't sure what made your mum more angry. The fact that you were playing Humpty or banging your head on the floor.' Emma chuckled and then added, 'You was off school for a week.'

'Partly due to concussion and feeling humiliated.' Barry did not enjoy reminiscing about this part of his life.

'So, how is your mum?' Emma continued excitedly.

'She died three years after that,' Barry replied.

Emma stopped giggling straight away and her face changed to one with full of concern, 'I am so sorry to hear that. You would have only been fifteen. You didn't have a dad around at the time, right?'

'No, he left my mum after I was born. After she died, I went to live with my aunt,' Barry explained.

Emma said nothing. She felt so ashamed that she had not even noticed that Barry had left school.

This time Barry was keen to change the subject and lighten the mood. 'You asked what I do for a living.'

'I imagine it must be something to do with computers. You look like a successful business type.' Emma couldn't help but be interested in learning more about him. She found him intriguing. Would she feel the same if he had not changed into such a devilishly handsome man? Deep down, she knew the answer to that.

Barry paused and grinned then proudly exclaimed, 'I'm a butler in the buff. It's my full time job.'

Emma gaped at him and tried to take in what he had just said. 'A what?'

'Butler in the buff. You know, I go to parties and wear nothing else but an apron and serve the guests.'

Emma glanced over his body and raised an eyebrow. 'Will you be giving us a demonstration later?' This was said more for comic effect but she did feel a little disappointed when he shook his head and said that he wouldn't.

Just at that moment, the doorbell rang and both of them turned towards the direction of where the sound was coming from.

'So, who is next to arrive?' Barry questioned cheerfully and made his way to the door. Emma waited in the kitchen. She was surprised with herself for feeling excited about the prospect of seeing her old school acquaintances again and wondered in anticipation if it would be Sarah, Jim or Rachael or perhaps Danny to enter the room. She listened as Barry opened the door. The sound of the pelting rain grew louder and she could feel a cool wind rush through the corridor and into the kitchen. It caused goose bumps to appear on her arms and as she subconsciously rubbed them, a shiver run through her body.

'Come in, quickly. It's absolutely ghastly out there today. Jim and Sarah? Still good friends I see,' Barry spoke joyfully.

'Barry? No way! You have changed so much and for the better. Get you!'

Emma instantly recognised Sarah's voice. She was still using her odd little phrases.

'Emma's already here. She arrived by taxi earlier on.' Barry's footsteps grew louder as he made his way back to the kitchen. Two sets of footsteps followed behind.

As the three of them came through the doorway, Emma sat up straight and gave a huge smile. Jim and Sarah looked first at the wheelchair and realizing what they were doing, focused on Emma's face. Their smiling faces could not hide their pity.

Barry sprinted over to the table and began to pour a drink for the two new arrivals and while refilling his own asked Emma if she would like another one too. She lifted her glass and passed it to Barry.

'You look fantastic,' Jim said to Emma.

'Thanks. You both look fantastic too. I can't believe how long it has been since we last spoke,' Emma responded.

'Ever since your accident really,' Jim replied thoughtfully.

Sarah smacked him on the arm and said, 'Jim, don't just come out with things like that. Emma probably doesn't want to talk about it.'

Emma quickly responded by saying, 'It's fine, please. I couldn't bare it if everyone had to tiptoe around the subject, petrified of saying something wrong.'

'I totally agree Emma,' Barry joined in while handing out the glasses. 'So, Jim, were we right? Do you bat for the same team?'

Jim gasped and opened his mouth in mock surprise. 'Now that is shocking and we haven't even finished our first drink. Anyway, no one uses that term anymore.'

Sarah frowned. She knew how nervous Jim was about touching on that subject and yet he hid it so well. She decided to join him in the same light hearted way, 'I'll tell them. Yes he's gay and desperate for a boyfriend.'

'I am not desperate.' Jim pouted as if pretending to be annoyed and lightly smacked Sarah on the arm. He paused, giving her a look that only she would understand. It showed his appreciation for helping him to keep the subject from getting too serious. He hoped that they could now move on without the need for intrusive questions.

'Barry fancy giving it a try?' Sarah continued.

'Not my kind of thing. Sorry,' Barry retorted very quickly and firmly.

After this, to Emma's surprise, the conversation changed within seconds, degenerating back to the old school days when they constantly mocked each other. She was no longer the centre of attention and felt more relaxed in her present company. All her anxieties and fears melted away and she began to enjoy the pleasant atmosphere that filled the room. Jim always had the gift of making those around him feel at ease. It was good to see that he never lost his charming ways. She hoped that when Rachael and Danny arrive, they would be equally as easy to get on with. So far, she had no regrets about accepting the invite and even the strange taxi driver drifted to the depths of her mind, filed away and forgotten.

'So, what do you do Emma?' Sarah asked.

Replying bashfully, she said, 'Me? Oh nothing much. I moved out from my parents' house to live alone in a flat and work for a local supermarket.'

'See, even Emma has moved out of her parents' place. Sarah here, still lives at home. Probably will still do so when she's eighty,' Jim spoke mockingly.

'What do you mean *even Emma?* That's not nice,' Sarah shouted back at him. Even though they both tried to sound as though they were angry, they grinned at each other mischievously. Emma wished she had a friendship with someone like theirs.

'Please, have something to eat. You must all be feeling peckish after your journey. Dinner will be served about 9ish. Hopefully, there should be something for everyone to enjoy,' said Barry.

'Boy, this does look good,' Sarah remarked and gawped at the table. As she reached for a sausage roll, Jim could not help himself but remind her that she was on a diet.

She turned to him and happily informed him, 'Not this weekend. It would be rude to our host if I didn't eat his food.' She then popped the sausage roll into her mouth and chewed it with relish. Jim just shook his head and chuckled.

'I love your hat,' Emma commented.

'This thing? I made it myself. It is the warmest and most cosy hat ever created,' Sarah exclaimed contentedly.

'It never comes off her head. I bet she sleeps with it on.' Jim grumbled and then swiped the hat and hid it behind his back.

Smoothing her hair down, Sarah remarked, 'I don't always wear it, just when it's cold.'

'Which in England, it means all the time. I rest my case,' Jim added with a cheeky smile and a wink at Emma.

'I'll show you to your rooms in a minute so that you can settle in properly.' Barry was keen to keep his guests happy. He was so pleased at how well things were going and was already starting to like all of his guests that had come so far.

'How many rooms are there in this place? It's huge.' Sarah was impressed. 'I love how you have decorated the kitchen. From what I could see from the corridor, the lounge looks just as good.'

'To be honest, I've only just done it. It was my aunt's house and since she passed away, I have been living in London,' Barry told them truthfully.

'God, if I had this, I would move in straight away.' Sarah said this without giving any consideration towards Barry's emotional feelings on the matter.

'It is a lovely house,' Emma whispered almost intimately to Barry.

'There are six double bedrooms. Four of them have en suites. There are also two further family bathrooms so there are enough of them to accommodate all of you. I don't mind which bedrooms you choose to stay in with the exception of the first one on the left. That's my room.' Barry spoke with the confidence and pride as the owner and master of the beautiful mansion.

'Sounds fantastic.' Jim was very impressed. He then looked in Sarah's direction and said with an element of sarcasm, 'I am sure whichever room I choose for myself, it will no doubt be the one Sarah will want.'

Sarah quickly replied, 'Only because you will want the best one as usual.'

'Barry organised a downstairs room for me,' Emma added.

'I am really looking forward to our time together. Barry, what a great idea of yours,' said Jim with enthusiasm.

'Yeah, I wasn't sure at first, I mean, it is weird that someone would make contact like that, out of the blue… but, yeah, I got a really good feeling about this weekend,' Sarah said eagerly.

CHAPTER TEN

Jim leaned forward with his hands on the bay window sill. His head almost touched the glass and as he breathed out, a mist formed on the window and then faded away. He stared intently at the landscape which was absolutely stunning with the natural world tumbling within the confines of the spacious garden and beyond. Unfortunately, the effect was ruined by the wretched storm that had broken the branches from the big, old trees and scattered the twigs and leaves that had fallen to the ground. The heavy rain and the vicious wind left a trail of devastation and death to nature's gifts of beauty and delight. Pools of muddy water drowned the thick, green grass but some blades managed to rise above it and peep out. Jim let out a heavy sigh and muttered, 'It is so depressing and gloomy out there.'

Sarah emerged from the en suite, drying her wet, thick, long dark hair with a towel. The droplets fell onto her dressing gown and were immediately absorbed by the thick, soft material. Her face was slightly flushed from just getting out of the shower. This gave her a healthy glow that enhanced her youthful and natural beauty. She also managed to maintain her shapely figure, even though she refused to exercise after she stopped dancing. Nevertheless, even though Sarah was the epitome of loveliness, she found it difficult to form a long relationship with a man, mainly because they never felt comfortable in her company. She always managed to somehow push them away. Every relationship that she had soon ended with the words, 'Let's just be friends, eh?'

She had tied her dressing gown as tightly as possible but was very aware of how short it was. The hem ended where her legs began and even though Jim would not have blinked if she was naked, she still felt uncomfortable. She tugged the hem line several times before reaching for her hairbrush.

'Why aren't you in your room? Shouldn't you be getting ready?' She hoped that he would leave so that she could prepare for dinner.

Jim turned towards her quickly and smiled, 'When you look as good as me it never takes long to get ready.' Then turned back to the window. 'I was saying how grim it is out there. The sky is the colour of dirty mustard.'

'Well, at least it has stopped raining.' Sarah placed her brush back on the table. 'What time do you think Danny or Rachael will get here? It can't be too long before we are called to dinner. Whatever is cooking sure smells appetising.'

'I think Barry mentioned something about them coming together.' Jim raised his eyes questioningly. 'Do you remember much about them?' Saying this, Jim moved towards the bed and sat down on the edge. He gently bounced up and down twice and was impressed by the softness of the mattress.

Sarah frowned and sat next to him and once more pulled at the hem of her dressing gown. Slowly, she shook her head, 'Not much. Danny was a bit weird and made me cringe.'

'Yeah, I know what you mean. Didn't he have a crush on Rachael at one point?' Jim's mind drifted to the past.

Sarah sneered in disgust, 'I don't know, I wanted nothing to do with him and neither did Rachael, no one did.'

Jim grew serious and his voice softened, 'I do remember one time, some of the lads beat him up in the playground. It was so brutal that it took the caretaker ages to clean the blood off the pavement.'

Sarah was shocked, 'I don't recall anything like that happening. Where was I at the time?'

Jim looked at his friend and his face was firmly set. 'You walked straight past as if nothing was going on.'

'I don't remember doing that,' Sarah whispered to herself.

'I have never known anyone to hate someone so much as you hated Danny.' Jim did not mean to be quite so blatant but his words sliced like a sharp knife into Sarah. She flinched but said nothing.

Seeing the look on her face, Jim tried to reassure her, 'Hey we were kids. Besides I hated him for joking about my sexuality. It was difficult for me to deal with it at that time.'

Sarah stared at Jim for a moment and then got up. She took the brush again and tugged it with all her strength to get the knots out from the ends of her hair. After a moment of silence she said, 'Rachael was a stuck up cow.'

Jim looked up at Sarah and was speechless. He had no idea that she felt so strongly about Rachael.

'She thought that she was all that,' Sarah continued.

Jim's brow furrowed as he listened and watched her shredding the final knots out of her hair. 'I thought you used to hang around with her.'

'That's when I realised what she was really like.' Sarah turned and pointed the hairbrush at Jim. 'Once, she tore up a Christmas card during tutorial. She threw the pieces in the air and laughed, shouting that she would never take anything from him. I don't know who the card was from but whoever it was must have been really upset about it. Now that's what I call a nasty piece of work.'

Jim replied thoughtfully, 'I think Danny gave her that card.'

'No way, really?' Sarah's eyes grew wide and a wicked grin slithered across her lips, 'And they are both coming here for the weekend. How awkward.'

'Funny that they should be arriving together though,' Jim added.

Both remained silent for a moment; both deep in their own thoughts. Sarah put the hair brush down and opened her make-up bag. Jim merely looked down at his hands, his lips slightly pouting and the furrow on his forehead became more pronounced. Then he spoke; more to himself than to Sarah, 'It's all very strange. All of us brought together like this. It seems that in some way we all touched on each other's lives and not only by being in the same tutor group. We all did something that seems so unpleasant now.'

Sarah glanced at Jim's reflection in the mirror and smirked, 'That is either very deep or melodramatic.'

'Admit it Sarah, you didn't want to accept the invitation in the first place. You only did it for me.'

Sarah felt her cheeks redden but did not deny what Jim had said.

Jim commented wistfully, 'I'm starting to wonder what Barry is up to. Why ask us here at all? I never really got on with him when we were at school. There was something odd about him. He seems alright now but you just never know what lurks beneath the surface.'

'There are lots of reasons why I asked you all to come here but something sinister is not one of them.' Barry was in the doorway. His head was slightly dipped and his hands were in his pockets.

'How long have you been standing there?' Sarah was mortified and started to pull the hem of her dressing gown again.

'Long enough,' Barry answered curtly. 'If you don't want to stay you can just leave. I'm not holding you prisoners. I will admit that at first my motives were selfish. I wanted to show you how much I changed in appearance and how I moved up in the world. Then I realised that none of that mattered when everyone invited here were the kindest to me at school and hence I became very pleased with the thought of seeing you all again.'

'But we never really spoke to you,' Sarah replied.

'Oh believe me, that was being kind. None of you laughed or jeered at me.' Barry lowered his head and bit his lip indicating that the past still troubled him.

Jim looked across to Sarah with a pained expression because he felt terrible about what he had said about Barry. Sarah looked back at him in the same way as she too felt extremely uncomfortable with the situation.

Finally Jim spoke and said, 'We are pleased to be here, honestly. It just feels odd reminiscing on the past like this. It kind of makes you realise that you have a different perspective of what happened back then.'

Barry's face lit up, 'I know what you mean but that's what makes it all so exciting. We don't know what is going to happen this weekend.' With this, Barry motioned that he had to run back downstairs and swiftly withdrew from the doorway.

Sarah and Jim looked at each other and shrugged their shoulders.

'Now that was embarrassing. I think we must be careful what we say. You don't know who might be listening,' Sarah whispered as she checked that the hallway was empty and that Barry had, indeed gone downstairs.

'See what I mean about being strange?' Jim spoke softly but firmly.

There was a knock on the front door and Sarah poked her head as far as she could over the stairs out of curiosity from seeing who arrived. All she could see was the top of Barry's head as he made his way to the front door while wiping his hands in a dish cloth. The wall blocked her view from seeing anything so she listened intently if she could hear what was being said.

'Ah! Danny and Rachael, you made it. Please come in, it's freezing out there.' Barry's voice sounded cheerful and friendly.

'Traffic was hell. It didn't help that darling Rachael here does not know the meaning of the word organised, otherwise we would have been here much sooner,' Danny answered with a deep, nasal voice. It was the kind of sound that would grate on the most patient person after a while. His tone was brusque, unfriendly and clearly showed that he was annoyed.

The only reason Sarah knew that Rachael was there because Barry and Danny had said her name. So far, she had remained completely silent even refraining from greeting her host. Sarah could not believe that Rachael could be so silent as she was always the first to start a conversation. As they made their way towards the stairs, Sarah quickly, closed the door and turned towards Jim who was watching her all this time.

'They both came together and he called her darling. Oh my God, are they a couple?' she whispered perhaps a bit too loudly.

Sarah placed her head against the door and listened. She could hear their footsteps walk past her bedroom and head towards the end of the corridor. Carefully, she opened the door but just enough to peep out to see Barry opening the bedroom door at the end of the corridor. She viewed it herself earlier and knew that it was the second largest in the house.

'I think this room will suit you both. The bed is specially made and larger than the normal king-sized ones. Please refresh yourselves and then you can meet everyone downstairs in time for dinner,' Barry informed the two arrivals.

'What time will we be expected?' Danny asked.

'Oh, just turn up when you are ready.' Barry chuckled.

'No, I need a specific time. What time are we expected?' Danny's tone was verging on the aggressive.

Barry's face dropped but he tried to remain calm out of politeness for his guests, 'Okay in that case, 9pm.'

Sarah could only see the back of Danny and Rachael but by the way they were standing, she could see that Danny was in charge. Although short, he seemed large in stature. Rachael's slight frame appeared awkward as she clutched her hands in front of her and head tilting downwards. This only stressed how thin she had become and the lack of confidence since the last time Sarah had seen her. Gone was the loud, positive, stuck up little girl that she used to know. Rachael was now a mere shadow of her former self with the vulnerability of fading to nothingness.

Sarah closed the door as quietly as she could, then facing Jim she said, 'I think this weekend will be very interesting.'

Jim said nothing but simply got up and patted his friend on the shoulder. He could see that she was physically shaken by what she had just seen. He was curious to know what had just occurred outside in the corridor but felt that now was not the time to quiz Sarah about it. He was sure that when she was ready to share her observations, she would. If not, he would find out for himself soon enough. He then opened the door and left to get ready for dinner.

Sarah placed her hand on his arm to stop him, 'Knock for me before you go downstairs. I don't want to meet them alone.'

Jim nodded then slipped out of the door.

After closing Sarah's door, he turned swiftly towards his room but halted as he could hear a muffled cry coming from Danny's and Rachael's room. He listened for a moment and then quietly tip-toed towards their door. He placed his ear just inches away from it and puckered his brow with concentration. The weeping sound was clearer and full of pain. Jim could tell that it was Rachael sobbing and desperately trying to stop.

Jim could hear Danny's angry voice saying, 'Bloody stop it. I can't stand your whining.'

'I'm sorry. I didn't mean anything by it,' Rachael lamented through her sobs.

'I saw the way you ogled at him. First bloke you see and you turn into a tart,' Danny hissed vehemently.

'I didn't, honest. I love you. This weekend is meant to be perfect for us,' Rachael wailed bitterly.

There was a thump like someone dropping to the floor and then Danny's voice shouting out, 'Get off my leg. You look pathetic when you get like this. Let go and sit down for God's sake. Stop clinging on to me.'

'Please, don't be like this,' Rachael whimpered.

'Oh yes, great weekend. You spoil everything.' Danny's voice sounded like that of a spoilt child.

'Oh darling, please don't say that,' Rachael pleaded.

'Come here.' Jim could hear the change in Danny's voice. It had calmed down and was almost soothing. There was something ugly and false about the way he manipulated the use of emotion in his tone. 'Come here!' This time it was more of a command.

There was a moment of silence.

'Stop crying, your eyes are getting puffy. Clean yourself up and look beautiful for me. I want the others to see what a prize I have.'

Jim grimaced and not wanting to hear anymore, stepped away from the door and promptly made his way to his own room. What he heard made him feel physically sick. He found it difficult to understand Rachael. Had she lost her self respect by allowing a man to treat her so badly and still beg for his forgiveness? Perhaps that is what happens to people when they are deeply and obsessively in love. As he moved, he glanced at Sarah's door. His face softened and his heart was filled with a protective kind of love. At that moment, he vowed that he would never let any man treat his friend in such a way, even if he had to drag her away kicking and screaming.

CHAPTER ELEVEN

Emma was the first guest to enter the dining room. She could not wait to see what Barry had in store for them all, therefore, wheeled herself in briskly. He was full of surprises that it became an expectation that something marvellous was planned for the evening. Her smile was bright and dream-like and she was excited and yet quite nervous. Her hair had been styled into delicate waves that bounced off her shoulders and flowed down her back. Her make-up was subtle but perfectly enhanced her features. She looked stunning and for the first time in a long time, she felt good about herself.

She gazed around the room and was in awe of every single detail that she saw. The electric lights were dimmed enough to allow the flicker of soft candlelight to illuminate the room. The huge log fireplace had been lit and the warmth that radiated from it took hold like a lover's embrace. Emma closed her eyes and bathed in the ambiance of the room which was peaceful and soothing.

After a little while, she opened her eyes and breathed in the scent of fresh perfume intertwined with the smell of the burning logs. She looked at the grand table which stood in the centre of the spacious room and noticed that it was adorned with candles and a vase containing yellow roses, the symbol of friendship. Emma was sure that they were chosen by Barry, so that their colour would be significant for the occasion and pleasing to the eye. Silver cutlery and plain white plates were placed on a white linen table cloth with a folded card containing a name, placed on each plate for the seating arrangement. Manoeuvring herself around the table, she read each card. Danny and Rachael were placed opposite each other across the table. Sarah was on Rachael's side opposite Jim. Her heart leapt when she saw her name opposite Barry who took the head of the table. Gently, she touched the card and followed the letters of her name. Each individual card was hand written. Everything was set out according to formal dining etiquette which showed the level of importance Barry held towards his guests. Her smile broadened. She was right; Barry did have something special planned.

Emma grinned shyly as she thought of Barry. He appeared to be responding to her flirtations and she knew that she was already falling for him. Strangely enough, this filled her with a new found confidence and the experience made her feel alive. What was more important, she felt like a beautiful, seductive woman that could snare the charming and handsome Barry. This was something that she never expected to happen. Her smile suddenly disappeared as she wondered if Barry could really have any feelings for her that went beyond friendship?

'Emma, you look absolutely amazing.' Barry had entered the room whilst Emma was deep in her thoughts. He gazed at her, unable to put into words what he truly wanted to say. His job introduced him to women without any dignity or shame. This led him to believe that all women were the same. Therefore, the sight of Emma's sheer innocence and simplicity completely stunned and baffled him.

Emma quickly turned towards Barry with a beaming smile, equally impressed by what she saw. He was dressed in a dinner suit which made him look elegant and even more dashing than ever. His mesmerising blue eyes shone vibrantly in the candlelight and his full lips tilted upwards at the corners of his mouth, giving him the appearance of a bashful smile. She could feel her cheeks turning red and averted her gaze towards the fireplace.

'I am so pleased to see you smile,' Barry commented. 'It is a lovely smile and perhaps suggests that you are happy to be here now.'

Emma turned back to face Barry, 'Oh Barry, it wasn't you. I was jittery because of that damn taxi driver, you know that. Yes, I am happy to be here, very happy.'

An awkward silence crept into the room and they both stared in different directions. Emma returned to the hypnotic dance of the flames in the fireplace whilst Barry studied the floor beneath him. There was so much that they wanted to say but did not know how to begin.

'Have you ever had a girlfriend?' She immediately regretted asking him this as it somehow sounded so silly now.

'Emma, you have to understand that in my line of work you see so much filth in women that it revolts you to the point of not being able to trust or even want a woman.' Barry explained all too frankly.

'Your Mother was a woman,' Emma shot back sharply. Even though his honesty was refreshing, it was not what she wanted to hear.

Barry physically flinched and then replied, 'Yes, and so was my auntie and I loved them both with my whole being.'

Emma looked up at him. Her expression was a mixture of sympathy and apology. The last thing that she wanted to do was wound him.

'Look Emma, I am enthralled by you and feel as though...' Barry was interrupted by Danny striding into the room. He was muttering under his breath about something. Behind him followed Rachael, who stared at Danny's back with a troubled expression. As soon as she saw there were other people in the room she forced a smile and straightened her posture.

Danny shuffled straight up to Barry. As he moved, he glanced at Emma with his usual sideways manner and then let his eyes roam around the room. 'We have arrived on time but I see two of the guests are late.' He boomed in a staccato rhythm that was smothered with impatience.

Barry, frustrated by the interruption, sounded agitated as he spoke, 'I am sure that Sarah and Jim will be here in a moment.'

Emma gave him a reassuring smile and he relaxed immediately. She too was very upset that Barry could not finish what he was about to say. Her stomach knotted with excitement at the thought that Barry was interested in her. Honestly, she could think of better words to use than 'enthralled' but it was an embarrassing moment and when she considered it a bit more, it was rather a sweet thing to say.

Rachael stepped to Danny's side. She lifted her hand towards his shoulder but thought better of it and returned it to its original position.

'Please take your seats. I am sure that I can hear Sarah and Jim coming. If you could excuse me for a moment so that I can check on the starter.' Barry peered once more at Emma. He found it almost impossible to pull his eyes away from her as she was so radiant. Then he walked out of the room and back into the kitchen.

'Emma, I presume.' Danny's eyes roamed up and down her body then settled on the wheelchair. Emma was aware of this but it no longer bothered her or made her feel uncomfortable. In fact, she did not care what was going on in his mind at that moment because her concern was more for Rachael, who was looking very frail.

'Sorry I was in my room when you both arrived. So, are you married?' Emma asked inquisitively. The match seemed ridiculous to her, especially from what she knew about them when they were younger.

'Partners,' Danny informed her. He took hold of Rachael's hand and placed it on his arm. As he patted her hand gently, Rachael smiled and glanced up at Danny lovingly. 'Bet you think I am a lucky man to have this pretty thing, eh?'

'That was exactly what I was thinking,' Emma answered with complete honesty.

'I am the lucky one really,' Rachael spoke in a quiet voice.

'No, I wouldn't say that,' Emma told her without hesitation. She could clearly see what kind of relationship they had and the mere thought of it made her shudder.

'What wouldn't you say Emma?' Sarah had entered the room. Jim was just behind her.

Danny seized the opportunity of belittling Rachael and putting her back into her place after Emma's unforgivable comments against him by saying, 'Rachael was just expressing how lucky she is to have me as a partner. Emma, I find your response a little rude as she is extremely fortunate to have me.' His tone was jovial but the way his nose flared as he glared at Emma made it clear that he was grossly offended by her.

Sarah's smile fell and Jim protectively linked his arms with hers and said, 'Danny, Rachael, it is good to see you both again.' He spoke without emotion but wanted to break the tense atmosphere that was in the room.

'Rachael would have died if it was not for me,' Danny continued.

Rachael's face filled with horror and she whispered, 'Danny please, don't.'

Ignoring her, Danny's voice grew louder, accentuating every syllable, making sure that every word was understood, 'You see, Rachael was a pitiful creature really. All of her past boyfriends used her as a punch bag.'

'Not all of them Danny,' Rachael argued pathetically.

'One in particular was in the process of beating her to death when I happened to be walking past. I got rid of him and then rushed her to hospital.' Danny's proud smirk was unsettling.

'That is just awful.' Jim screwed up his face in disgust.

Rachael was distraught. 'You shouldn't have told them Danny. I begged you not to.'

Danny's grin widened. 'It's okay my delicate flower, I am sure much will be shared by all tonight.'

Barry entered the room holding a bottle of sherry and placed it on the dining table. He began to collect some glasses from the sideboard, 'I hope everyone is content to chat and have a drink while I finish off the starter?'

No one answered but Barry was not at all surprised as he could feel the tension as soon as he walked into the room. He chose not to confront the situation but quietly filled the glasses with sherry and handed them out. 'There is a choice of vegetable soup or melon with strawberries as the vegetarian option, smoked salmon mouse or venison pate.'

Danny was first one to answer. 'I'll have the venison pate and Rachael will have the melon. She is always on a diet of some kind.'

Sarah huffed at this comment but Danny chose to ignore it.

'I will have the salmon please.' Jim was far more polite in his response.

Sarah asked for the same starter as Jim.

'Could I have the soup please?' Emma asked.

Barry smiled gently at her and said that he too would be having the soup.

Before long, everyone settled and with every course, the conversation flowed more easily. Before long, they were reminiscing on the positive aspects of the good old days. They shared thoughts about past teachers and their lessons as well as school trips that they went on. Even Rachael's mood seemed to improve as she felt able to relax a little bit in the safe company of so many people. She joined in and entertained the rest of the group with tales of the antics that she got up to, some of which they did not know about. However, she still remained very careful not to say anything that would displease Danny. From the corner of her eyes, she could see that he was watching and monitoring every movement and word that she said.

'Barry, the meal was absolutely delicious.' Sarah stared at her empty plate and put her spoon and fork down.

Barry beamed with pride; the evening had gone well so far, 'Would you like some more wine?'

'Oh don't let her have any more,' Jim joked, 'she becomes impossible when she drinks and I am positive that she is already a bit tipsy.'

'It is true that it goes straight to my head but I'm not impossible, just a little light headed. And yes please, I will have another drink, why not?' She took the bottle from the centre of the table and filled her glass and then turned towards Rachael, swaying the bottle over her empty goblet.

Danny stiffened, showing his disapproval. Rachael was aware of his reaction and quickly raised her voice in panic, 'Oh, no thank you!' Danny relaxed back into his chair and smiled at Rachael, satisfied with her response.

'All the more for me,' Sarah chirped, raising an eyebrow at Jim, knowing that he was also aware of the reason why Rachael declined the drink.

'So Sarah, I think it is fantastic that you are an artist. Jim tells me that you are very talented.' Emma smiled with enthusiasm.

Taking a swig of wine, Sarah nodded, 'Yes, I didn't even know myself for a long time. I found out by accident.'

'Like most things in life,' Emma commented quietly.

Sarah stared at Emma, trying to work out what she meant by that. She filled her glass once more even though Jim frowned at her.

'Danny, I hear that you have a very respectable job as an Accountant. Fair play to you,' Barry cut in.

Danny turned towards Barry and grinned, 'Yes I have. I am hoping for promotion later this year.'

Rachael sat up straight and clapped her hands, 'Darling, that's wonderful. You didn't tell me.'

'I don't always tell you everything,' Danny replied. His tone was good humoured but Rachael was clearly hurt by his answer. She put her head down and remained silent.

Sarah finished her glass and again reached for the bottle. She held it up and saw that it was empty. She placed it back on the table and glanced at Barry who chose to ignore her. Everyone could see that she had more than enough. 'Emma, I must ask, what did you mean when you said earlier on, like most things in life? What were you trying to say?'

Emma lifted her head and looked alarmed; she hated any form of confrontation. She swept her eyes across the table and settled them on Sarah, 'I didn't mean anything by it, really.'

'Then why say it?' Sarah was adamant to have her question answered.

'I just think that sometimes things happen to change the course of our life, that's all,' Emma responded, trying to be tactful in her choice of words. Obviously, the wine was making Sarah paranoid.

'Like the reason why you are in a wheelchair?' Sarah's words made Emma flinch. 'If I had danced that night, you wouldn't have been crushed between two cars. Is that what you were thinking?'

Emma felt anger churn inside of her but tried to remain calm.

Sarah continued to interrogate Rachael, showing no mercy. 'I bet you wish that I had been the one on the stage that fateful night instead, just to prevent the miserable life you ended up with?'

Jim's frown deepened and he was about to say something. However, what came next happened so quickly that everyone around the table gasped in surprise. Emma shouted, 'Perhaps I do, is that what you wanted to hear?'

Sarah stood up and grabbed Jim's drink and threw it at Emma's face from across the table. It splashed over Emma's dress and dripped onto her lap. For a moment, it was as if time stood still and everyone froze, forming a gruesome tableau. Barry held both hands to his forehead and closed his eyes. Jim glared up at Sarah with his lips tightly pressed together. Rachael had her mouth wide open, expressing shock and disbelief. Danny merely smiled, beguiled by the performance. Sarah was the only one moving. She breathed heavily and her hand that was holding the glass shook uncontrollably. Time moved when she let go of the glass and it fell, shattering loudly on the floor.

Barry ran around the table to Emma and gave her a napkin to wipe her face while Jim shouted at Sarah across the table. Rachael and Danny remained seated and watched all the commotion in silence.

'I am so sorry, truly so sorry,' Sarah whined on the verge of tears. The incident had seemed to sober her up somewhat.

Jim looked at his friend with a pained expression and lowered his voice. He moved close to her and put an arm around her shoulder. Turning to the rest of them, he mumbled, 'I think it best if I take Sarah to her room.' Slowly, he coaxed her into moving towards the door without making eye contact with anyone.

After a moment, Emma wheeled herself out of the room, whimpering quietly. Those who remained watched her leave without a word. They appreciated the fact that she felt humiliated and needed some time alone.

'I hope that you will still crack open the cognac as promised Barry?' Danny announced as if nothing had happened. 'Rachael, go to bed. You need to rest after such an eventful day.'

Rachael glanced at Barry wanting to say something but unable to find the right words, kissed Danny on the cheek and plodded unsteadily out of the room.

CHAPTER TWELVE

As soon as Emma had closed the door of her room, tears of frustration began to fall down her cheeks. She could not believe how quickly things could change from an exciting and eventful evening to one of humiliation and great disappointment. Not more than an hour ago, for once in her life, she had felt as though she was floating on air. It had appeared that fortune finally found her and was smiling from above. She had dared to believe that there was a chance for a better future filled with love, happiness and above all companionship. Within moments, Sarah had caused it all to come crashing down with the snap of her evil, drunken tongue.

The way she felt right now was not because Sarah threw the wine in her face as she could have dealt with that. There were many occasions when Emma had to face nasty behaviour from ignorant people. What really hurt her was seeing the horrified expression on Barry's face as she looked towards him for help. He closed his eyes as if he did not want to look at her. How could he possibly believe that she would ever wish Sarah a 'miserable life'? Sarah was demanding an answer and she was not going to stop until she got one. Being at the centre of all the screaming and shouting, made Emma feel sick with panic. When her nerves finally snapped, the answer she gave was misunderstood by everyone in the room and not at all what she meant it to be. If Sarah had danced that evening instead of her, then the accident would not have happened to either of them. The situation would have been very different. As it so happened, the cruel side of fate resulted in her not being able to walk again. It was meant to be but she would never have wished it on anyone, especially Sarah. Emma leaned her head against the door, closed her eyes and began to weep.

Suddenly, a knock on the door startled her. She straightened up and moved away from the door, staring at it. Then, another soft knock. 'Emma, please... I just want to know if you are alright.' It was Barry. His voice was full of concern and yet Emma was not sure if it was out of pity or the obligation of a polite host. Either way, she didn't want it. She was sick of people's pity and their need to justify their actions. Anyway, it was certainly not what she wanted from Barry. She remained quiet and waited for him to leave. After a few moments, she could hear his footsteps making their way across the corridor and then a sound of a door closing. Emma was feeling very bitter and needed the time to think.

Slowly, she made her way to the bathroom, which was luckily connected to the study. She had no intention of bumping into anyone and was grateful that she did not have to go out into the main corridor. In fact, at that moment in time, she felt that she would rather die than face any of them again.

After washing the wine out of her hair and from her face, she prepared for bed. She gazed upon her reflection in the mirror and saw a plain girl stare back with a vacant expression. How could she ever think that she was attractive? How stupid of her. She turned away from the girl in the reflection and switched off the bathroom light. Wheeling herself to the side of the bed, she paused for a moment, staring at the welcoming bed. Sleep had always been the one place where she could get away from all the vile and unpleasantness of life. Once it enveloped her into its nothingness, she found herself in a place which freed her from an unhappy state or sometimes into a world of dreams where she could walk again. Right now, that was the only thing she wanted; sleep. She left the wheelchair next to the bed, as she always did, and relaxed in the soft, warm bed. She was already starting to drift off when she felt a gentle breeze caress her shoulder. Its fingers were icy. Frowning, she pulled the duvet up to cover herself. Even though she was on the ground floor, she did not care that the window had been left slightly open. She did not care for anything but a long, peaceful slumber.

★

The moon shone brightly in the black sky. No stars were visible. The whole house was completely silent as everyone had finally gone to bed. Emma was immersed in the depths of sleep, oblivious to the chilly wind that swept into the room.

In the corner of the open window, a spider was finding its way into the room. Very cautiously, he placed his long leg over the edge of the frame. It was difficult to be nimble as he was rather big. With a leg span of fifteen centimetres and a body of forty eight millimetres, fitting into small spaces was a chore. However, self-preservation was the most important thing on his mind and this was new territory. It caused him to feel uncomfortable, vulnerable and very tense. The spider was not used to the conditions in the new surroundings that he had found himself in. The weather was wrong and the forest behind him looked pathetically small. On the ground, below the window, he watched how the other species of spiders and insects recoiled at the sight of him and ran off in terror. This spider was not concerned about these little creatures as they posed no threat to him. He was feared by larger insects than these, so their reaction humoured and kept him occupied for a while. There was something majestic and strong about him, and he knew it. True to his name, he liked to wander around. Web making was tiresome and he could not think of anything more boring than just sitting in a tree waiting for food to come to him. This spider preferred finding his own prey.

He slowly pulled himself up until his whole body was inside the room, immediately sensing that he was not alone. Something else was there and much bigger than him. The spider liked a challenge and whatever was in the room certainly gave off the scent of being a worthy victim. His brown skin and thick, dark brown hairs that covered all of his body were in stark contrast to the sheer whiteness of the window sill and so he decided to move further into the shadows. Dropping to the floor he scuttled across it and hid behind the back of the bed. Dust spilled into his mouth which annoyed him and he had to spend some time removing it with his front legs. It left a nasty taste in his mouth which irritated him further. He did not like this place at all.

Emma rolled over in her sleep and moaned. The sound was barely a whisper but the spider could hear it. By listening carefully, he could follow the slow rhythm of her breathing and found this intriguing. He decided to examine his prey before making a move. He had no interest in anything going on outside and was not particularly hungry, therefore, had all the time in the world to amuse himself. He would have a little adventure and perhaps, a little fun.

The duvet that had partially slipped down within an inch off the floor, made it easy for the spider to reach and climb up it. As the material was cotton, gripping was easy and within seconds he found himself on top of the bed. The victim's scent was stronger and the spider began his exploration. He watched the sleeping victim and studied the part of her that was not covered by the strange cocoon that she was wrapped in. He was fascinated with the hair that spread from the head across the pillow. It was silky and smooth but stronger than any web that he had ever seen before. Feeling brave, he tiptoed through the strands until he reached the other side of the pillow. Satisfied with his antics, the spider dared to venture further and scurried down towards Emma's cheek. A gust of wind bellowed out of her nostrils and so the spider decided to settle a bit further back for a while, next to her ear. The skin was warm and the tiny hairs felt ticklish and so the spider wandered across her face, over her nose before moving under the duvet.

Slowly, he followed the contour of his victim's body and as he got deeper towards the centre of the bed, it became unpleasantly hot. Of course, having come from South America, he was used to a hot climate but this was unbearable. It was damp and stifling. For the first time in his entire life, the spider began to worry and continued his journey in order to find his way back out into the fresh air.

Suddenly, Emma turned around again and the spider panicked. In fear of being crushed, he bit into his victim and injected every drop of venom that he had. Once spent, he scampered along the same path he had started until he found the end of the bed at Emma's feet. Without hesitation, he dropped to the floor and hurried back towards the window. He did not want to spend another minute in the room and so moved hurriedly back out of the house.

The spider had bitten Emma on her thigh. She was totally unaware of this as she had no feeling below the waist. The deadly venom slowly worked through her blood stream.

Later, when the sun was ready to emerge from the horizon and begin to throw light on the world, Emma woke up with a start. She was disorientated. Her whole body was screaming with excruciating pain. Her breathing was laboured and she was dripping with sweat. She clawed at the duvet with as much effort as she could muster, managing to throw it aside. Exhausted but determined, she reached for the wheelchair but could not find it. She was sure that she placed it next to the bed but for some reason it was not there. Barely able to lift her head, she turned and looked for it. The wheelchair was as least five feet further than where it was supposed to be and clearly beyond her reach. She did not have the energy to crawl to it and every movement caused the pain to intensify. Realising her predicament, she attempted to scream but not even a whimper escaped from her lips. To her torment and horror, it dawned on her that she was dying and there was nothing that she could do about it. No one would come to her rescue as she was completely powerless to scream for help. Her muscles were paralysed even in the upper part of her body and she was completely useless. No matter how wretched her life had been or would be in the future, she did not want to die. Her mind was filled with panic and urgently sought ways to cling on to the hope that this was not going to be the end. Her life could not end like this. Finally, after a short while, Emma realised the futility of her struggle and all that she could do was watch the sun in the sky for the last time. Fire burned in her throat as she tried with all her might to suck in a stream of air but she was no longer able to breath. Just as the sun was strong enough to send beams of light through the window, Emma had become too weak and died.

CHAPTER THIRTEEN

Barry woke up to the sun's rays filtering through the gaps in the blinds. He winced and rubbed his eyes, trying to coax them into opening. Barry groaned as he picked his head up from the pillow but only to fall back onto it again. His head was throbbing and his tongue felt too large for his mouth. He had drunk far too much the previous night and his system was not used to taking such a battering. It had been a long time since he had consumed such a disgusting amount of alcohol. He began to consider exactly how much he had. It started with a couple of Sherries, followed by four glasses of wine. That should have been fine considering the amount of food he had eaten. Then Danny's voice popped into his head, 'I hope that you will still crack open the cognac as promised, Barry?' That was where it all went wrong and he drank quite a few glasses of cognac on top of what he already had. That was why he was feeling so rough.

Then his thoughts turned to Emma. He could not forget the way she silently left the room and it broke his heart. Looking back on the evening, he knew that he should have immediately comforted Emma by putting his arms around her. It was all too late by the time he knocked on her door to ask if she was okay. No wonder there was no reply. By then everyone retired to bed except for Danny who was determined to get his cognac. He was in no mood to entertain but felt compelled to do so. Frustrated about what happened, he did not think about the amount of times he had filled his own glass. Danny continued to blabber on about his wonderful job not giving a thought as to what happened between the girls. Barry did think about trying to knock on Emma's door again but Danny remained seated until it was too late. She would have been fast asleep by then and he had no wish to disturb her. He thought that it would be for the best to leave things until morning when he could talk to Emma and explain why he was so slow in consoling her and hope that she would understand. Barry also wanted to tell her how he felt about her because he did not want to lose her.

As he was thinking back through the events that had taken place, he could not remember refilling Danny's glass after the first one. Danny certainly did not reach for the bottle at any time. He just seemed content to talk into the late hours of the night without the help of a few top ups. 'Wise man,' Barry mumbled to himself.

Slowly he turned to look at the clock. At first, his vision was blurry but after a few moments the numbers came into focus, 10:34 am. Without registering the time, he placed his head back on the pillow. Every time he tried to move, there was the feeling of a drill, digging into his head. In fact, his whole body ached. He must have slept deeply in a bad position and was now suffering the consequences. It was no good just laying there feeling sorry for himself so he turned his head towards the clock realising that it was already 10:36. Placing his hand over his face, he sighed. He intended to get up at 8 a.m. in order to have breakfast organised for his guests. He could only hope that everyone else had slept in.

He rubbed his forehead in agitation as he thought about the fight between Sarah and Emma. It was something totally unexpected. Even though it did not make any sense, he could not help but feel that Danny was somehow the cause of the conflict between the two girls.

He knew that his only option was to try again; he had to make it up to Emma. Hopefully, the new light of day would make things seem better and that the heated argument was just a silly, drunken row. After a good night's sleep there was a chance that everything could be brushed under the carpet and they all could start afresh.

After a quick shower and shave, he dressed casually in a pair of jeans and a dark blue t-shirt. Taking a deep breath, Barry went out into the corridor. Everything was silent. It appeared that he was the first to rise after all. Carefully, he sprinted down the stairs, straight to Emma's door. Pausing for a moment to compose himself, he ran his fingers through his hair. He was extremely nervous. Slowly, he curled his hand into a fist and gently rapped on the door. There was no answer. Once more, he knocked but more firmly. Something just did not feel right. The silence was eerie and made his spine chill. Again, there was no reply. Panicking, he began to hammer on the door and called out, 'Emma, Emma! Answer me. Are you okay? Emma!'

'No matter how angry or upset she might be surely she would come to the door?' Barry's mind was tumbling giddily with various thoughts. 'Maybe she is hurt and needs help?' However, there was a dark and frightening notion that preceded all others. 'What if something serious had happened?'

'Pack it in Barry, jeez my head hurts.' Sarah was half way down the stairs.

'It's Emma. She isn't answering the door. I think I should go in.' He spoke with urgency in his voice.

'Oh yeah, right. What if she is getting changed or just wants to be left alone?' Sarah yawned and clutched the side of her head. Her eyes looked like slits and she was extremely pale.

Barry took a key from the side drawer and with his hand shaking, opened the door.

The window was wide open and a gust of wind blew in his face. He blinked, surprised by its strength and then noticed that the bed looked as if no one had slept in it. There was no sign of Emma ever being there. He charged inside and went through to the bathroom and found that too was empty. There was no shampoo, perfume or even a toothbrush by the sink.

'Her clothes and bag are gone... oh, and her wheelchair of course.' Barry could hardly hear what Sarah was saying when she followed him into the bedroom.

With his head bowed in resignation, he left the bathroom and found Sarah still poking around the drawer on the side table. When she noticed him, she shut it and said, 'Do you think she left in the middle of the night? Surely someone would have heard her leaving?'

Barry glowered down at her, 'Did you even consider for a moment that if she has left, it is all because of you?' He brushed against her with the strength that made her unsteady on her feet and stormed out of the room.

Sarah was stung by his comment and ran after him. She followed until he stopped in the kitchen and took a bottle of water from the fridge. Staring at the garden through the window by the sink, he twisted the cap off the bottle and gulped several times. Sarah stood a little distance behind him and just watched quietly for a moment, allowing him time to calm down.

'She would have had to call for a taxi. Surely we would have heard the sound of the engine. I can't believe that she would go without talking to me first.' Barry was clearly hurt.

Sarah stepped a little closer towards him, 'I didn't mean for that to happen. It was a mistake.' She was close to tears.

Barry turned sharply, 'I don't want to hear your pathetic apologies or excuses, Sarah. Emma has gone and I doubt I will ever get to see her again. Do you find it fun to destroy everyone that you come in contact with? Jim must be a glutton for punishment. I bet you even ruined his relationship with Archie. Oh yes, everyone knew about his friendship with Archie. Word gets round and so does gossip. They got together didn't they and you had to make sure that it wouldn't last.'

Sarah winced at his accusation.

Barry realised he had stumbled on a secret that festered inside of her for all this time. 'Oh my God, you did, didn't you and I bet Jim doesn't even know? What was it, a quiet word in the ear? A subtle lie that spun out of control?'

Sarah froze to the spot and was unable to move let alone say anything in her defence.

'Give Emma time. She is just feeling a bit sore for now. You can't give up so easily. Everyone could see how well the two of you were getting on.' Said Sarah, trying to avoid answering Barry's questions about Archie. She was quite shaken by his discovery and how easy it was for him to stumble on the truth. It must have been written all over her face.

'For now, stay away from me. I don't want your advice, okay? Just keep out of my sight. You are filth.' Barry's icy glare made Sarah shiver and she stepped back.

'Hey, that's a bit harsh,' Jim said entering the kitchen, catching the tail end of the conversation. He didn't like the menacing tone of Barry's voice.

Barry turned his attention to Jim but felt it would be too cruel to tell him the truth about Archie. He genuinely liked him and did not see the point in opening up old wounds so he decided to keep Sarah's secret and let her live with the burden of having it on her conscience, that is if she had one. After the slight pause, he said, 'Emma left sometime before morning. She's gone.'

Jim automatically looked at Sarah and she knew that he also blamed her for Emma leaving. He was too loyal to say this and instead put his arm on her shoulder for comfort. Turning to Barry, he asked, 'What happens now?'

Barry had not considered this yet and so paused for a moment to think. 'Perhaps it would be best if we continue with the weekend as planned. I will try and call her later to find out how she is. With any luck, I might persuade her to come back.' He still clung to a glimmer of hope that he could convince her to return and yet the sad look on his face suggested he knew that he had lost her.

'I am glad to hear that.' Danny entered through the back door that led into the kitchen. He was wearing joggers and a t-shirt. His hair looked wet from sweat and his face was red. 'It isn't as though someone died you know.'

'Danny, that's a horrible thing to say,' said Sarah screwing up her face. She felt his comment was distasteful.

Danny merely shrugged his shoulders and replied, 'I am sure Emma will contact us when she is ready and that you will see her again Barry, don't worry.'

'Where have you been? It's freezing outside.' Jim frowned.

'The fresh air is good for you. I always have my morning run at the weekend.' Danny smiled smugly. 'Guess it's time to wake sleeping beauty now.' He looked up at the ceiling to indicate Rachael. 'I couldn't move her this morning.'

They were all amazed that nothing seemed to bother him and as Danny moved towards the corridor, the three of them watched him go.

Sarah turned to Barry, 'I guess I ought to go to my room and get out of your way.' This was said without any scorn. Before she even made it to the kitchen door, Barry called out, 'No, wait. You are still a guest in my house and I should not have behaved in that way.' He looked at Jim who was staring directly at him. Feeling uncomfortable with this, he averted his eyes and settled them on an empty sink. 'Anyway, it's not me who should have any real gripe with you. I am not your best friend.' The emphasis on the word 'best' created a sarcastic tone.

Without another word, Barry turned his attention to preparing breakfast. Jim frowned at Sarah then raised his eyebrows questioningly. Sarah shook her head and walked out of the kitchen. Deciding to ignore Barry's cryptic comment, he followed Sarah who was making her way into the lounge. He would ask her what it was all about later.

It was not long before Rachael and Danny joined them. Rachael looked rather dopey as though she had not fully woken up yet. Her head felt fuzzy and she was not aware of what she was saying, 'I can't believe I slept so late. I always get up early to make sure that your trainers are by the door. Please forgive me Danny. It won't happen again.'

Danny smiled, pleased that she was making a complete idiot of herself. He stroked her hair and soothingly muttered, 'It's okay Rachael, the journey was long and tiring.'

Sarah stared at him. Her lips were curled in disgust. There was so much she wanted to say to him but due to her performance last night and the trouble it caused, she chose to keep her opinions to herself.

'You are so good to me Danny,' Rachael's voice was barely audible yet her adoration for Danny was clear.

Sarah could not stand to be in the room and witness the mockery any longer. Rolling her eyes, she stood up and walked out. She began to head towards the kitchen but seeing Barry tapping a number on his phone, diverted and made her way back to her bedroom.

Sarah closed the door and sat on the bed, wondering how she gave herself away to Barry. It did not take him long to see right through her and discover her deceit. Now that he knew about it, how long would it take him before he told Jim?

At first, she thought that it would be unlikely that Jim's parents would accept his relationship with Archie but it did not take long before they welcomed him with open arms. Soon after, Jim began talking about sharing a flat with Archie as a couple. Sarah had not expected their relationship to develop so fast. She saw less of Jim and his family because he was spending most of his time with his partner. Sarah felt herself fading away into the background and she did not like it. Jim belonged to her and there was no way that she was going to let him go. They belonged together and no one was going to come between them. She knew that both Archie and Jim trusted her implicitly and this was her finest weapon. Sarah hatched a plan and all she had to do was wait for the perfect moment to execute it. It did not take long before the opportunity arose.

The three of them arranged to meet at the King's Head, a local pub. Archie was already there when Sarah arrived. He told her that Jim sent a text, letting him know that he would be a bit late. It was then that Sarah decided that it would be the right time to act and whisper poison into Archie's ear. She sat herself next to him, grabbed hold of his hand and looked solemnly into his face. She then told Archie that Jim had confided in her that he no longer had feelings for him and had no idea how to break the news. He still loved him as a special friend and was pleased that they shared happy times together. Archie helped him to come out, allowing him to be free and comfortable with being a homosexual. He would be eternally grateful to Archie for that but he felt trapped in their relationship. He was not ready to commit himself to one person yet and wanted to grab life in both hands and experience its adventures.

Sarah could remember the look on Archie's face as he stared at her searchingly with eyes that were imploring for guidance as to what he should do. She coolly said, 'I think it best you leave him. Just walk away. Long goodbyes are the most painful thing to go through. If you love him...'

'Let him go,' Archie finished the sentence for her.

She remembered feeling nothing for Archie, even as the tears spilled over his cheeks. She had cruelly destroyed him and gave no thought to the fact that she would be destroying Jim too. The only thought that was running through her brain was the satisfaction of getting her way. It was so easy.

Archie quietly vanished and Jim was left feeling confused and heartbroken. It was she who comforted him and stayed by his side. Since then, he was completely grateful for her friendship and patience.

At the time, she was incapable of any emotion or remorse.

It was not until many years later, that guilt crept in with the mellowness that comes with age, like a maggot, slowly crawling into her maturing mind and rotting away the obsessive need to control Jim. She began to understand that he would always be her true friend no matter what and she was grateful for his loyalty and kindness but could never reveal to him what she had done. If he ever found out about her evil secret, it would kill his love, trust and faith in her forever.

Jim opened the door without knocking and stood close to her with a very determined look on his face. Before Sarah could say a word, he launched into his speech, 'Sarah, I know there is something you are not telling me. When Barry spoke to you in the kitchen, I could see that there was some kind of strange understanding between both of you. Please, tell me what it is. It can't be that bad, even by your standards. If you really respect me as a friend, then you will tell me what it is that you are hiding from me. If you have anything to say, say it.'

Sarah opened her mouth and then closed it again and remained silent.

To her relief, Barry poked his head through the gap in the door, preventing Jim from pressing her further, 'I just wanted to say, breakfast is ready. By the way, Emma isn't answering her phone.'

Slowly, Barry turned and made his way back down the stairs. Jim turned back to Sarah vowing, 'Believe me, this conversation is not over.' Then he too, descended the stairs. After a moment, Sarah quietly followed.

CHAPTER FOURTEEN

Everyone sat in the same seats as the previous evening. It made Emma's vacant seat all the more noticeable. From time to time, Barry stared at it with a furrowed brow. To him, it was now a black, gaping hole when only a few hours ago, it was filled with light and warmth. He could clearly picture her throwing her head back gently and laughing. Her left hand touching her delicate throat and the right, wrapping its thin fingers around the sparkling chain around her neck. From time to time, she would peer over at him and smile shyly yet enticingly. In a sweet way, she invited him to surrender to her charms instead of forcing them on him. She was a woman unlike any other and now she was gone.

The table cloth had been changed and the stains in the carpet had been cleaned. If only it would be that simple as to wipe away the dreadful argument between Emma and Sarah and start all over again but this time without making any mistakes and keeping hold of the rare diamond, he found in Emma.

The spread that was perfectly set out across the table was lavish and pleasing to the eye. The aroma of freshly brewed coffee and orange juice waltzed in the air with the delicious smells of newly baked bread and toast. There were various assortments of cereals, cold meats, cheeses and fruits. The guests were spoilt for choice and yet the mood in the room was sombre.

Everyone around the table was haunted by the quarrel and how it ended. What bothered them the most was Emma's strange disappearance. As they chomped on the food, they silently contemplated as to why she left so discreetly. It made no sense.

No one spoke.

Jim kept looking across at Sarah, frowning and at times glaring angrily at the others. All his thoughts and feelings were in total disarray because he could not understand why it was so important for him to unearth Sarah's secret. He was determined to get her attention but she stubbornly avoided eye contact. Her head was bowed towards the table and she was solely focused on her plate and glass.

Rachael looked nauseous and picked at her food. Danny observed her now and again but did not seem to show any concern. As she picked up her cup of steaming coffee, her hand shook and so she placed it back on to the saucer. She gave an apologetic smile and was relieved to see that no one had noticed.

Once everyone had eaten, Barry got up and started to clear the table. Just as he picked up a couple of plates, Danny broke the silence by asking, 'So, what have we got planned for today?'

Barry stopped picking up the empty plates and looked at each of his remaining guests. All attention was on him as they all waited for his reply. It appeared that they were desperate to do something that would preoccupy their minds and forget what happened yesterday evening. They still had the rest of the weekend and were determined to make the most of it. Barry put down the crockery that he was holding in his hands back onto the table and took a deep breath. After a short pause, he said, 'My plan was for us to walk into town and browse around the shops. We could stop for lunch in this lovely little restaurant that I have been to on several occasions. After that, I was hoping to take a different route back to change the scenery and show you more of the surrounding area. There is a little stream in a nearby field, where borage grows in abundance. When the wind blows, the flowers form gentle waves, making the field look like the sea. It is beautiful there even at this time of the year.

'That sounds beautiful,' said Rachael with a little more zest. She loved the natural world, especially wild flowers and could not help but become interested with the thought of walking through a sea of blue petals.

Danny glimpsed across at Rachael and grinned, 'I'm impressed. I thought you were not well enough to go on any outings today. Are you sure you are up for it?'

Rachael wanted more than anything to go outside and breathe in the fresh air. She would welcome its bitter edge, inhaling deeply, allowing the coldness to clear her head. She stared at Danny and smiled wryly, 'I will manage, believe me.'

'Good girl!' Danny exclaimed loudly. 'Barry, that sounds wonderful.'

'I don't think I will join you, sorry,' Sarah remarked rather sharply. 'I would prefer to rest here if that's okay?'

'Of course,' Barry assured her with a warm smile on his face. 'Whilst you are here you can do whatever you like. Take anything you want from the kitchen when you get hungry or thirsty, anything at all. Make yourself feel at home.'

'Thanks. I think it would do me good to nurse my head,' Sarah explained.

Jim offering out of concern said, 'I'll stay with you.'

'No. That isn't necessary. You go out and enjoy the day. I'd rather be by myself. Thanks all the same,' Sarah replied brusquely.

Jim hesitated and opened his mouth to say something but decided against it when Sarah lifted her head and stared straight into his eyes. Her face was stern and full of determination. It was obvious that she wanted to be on her own and Jim knew her well enough to know not to press her on the subject. Respecting her wishes, he replied in a much calmer voice, 'As you wish but if you change your mind, please say.'

'Okay, so everyone is happy with the arrangements?' Barry was met with a few nods of agreement. 'Then, let's meet up in the lounge in half an hour. Please wear sturdy boots and wrap up warm. It may not be raining anymore but the wind is still strong.'

With this, everyone dispersed to prepare for the days outing.

Once everyone had left the room, Barry sat back down at the table and pulled his phone out of his jeans pocket. He pressed the key to redial Emma and listened to the hypnotic purr of the ringing tone. It went on for a long time before the voicemail cut in telling him that the person he is calling is not available. It then politely asked him to please leave a message after the tone.

Barry rubbed his forehead nervously as he heard the beep indicating that he should start talking. He began, 'Emma, it's me again. I don't mean to pressure you or anything. I just want to know that you are fine.' He paused to gain control of his voice as it began to crack with emotion. 'I will respect the fact that you may feel like you never want to see me again... for the moment, although I didn't think things were that bad. I really do think a lot of you and would do anything just to hear you say that you are okay. If you don't want to speak then just text.' Once more, he paused to find the right words, licked his lips and sat up, 'Listen, I feel as though I, I...' The sound of a beep indicated that he ran out of time and cut him off. He stared at the phone in his hand and then switched it off. 'Damn!' he whispered to himself. Slowly, he got up and made his way to his bedroom to get ready.

A little while later, Barry emerged from his room and sprinted down the stairs. When he reached the bottom, he could hear the sound of tinkering glasses coming from the kitchen and went in to investigate. He stood in the doorway and found Danny by the sink, filling a glass with water. Before he could say anything, Danny spun round to see who it was and gave his usual crooked smile before taking a sip of the water. He put the glass down on the counter and stated jovially, 'I thought I could hear someone creeping up behind me.'

'You must have sharp ears,' Barry commented. 'I wasn't creeping up on you anyway. Hey, there was spring water placed in your room yesterday. Do you need more?'

Danny waved his hand absently, 'Don't trouble yourself. Rachael was rather thirsty and drank it all. I don't mind the tap stuff. It's never done me any harm.' Danny seemed to find this amusing and chuckled to himself.

'You seem to be in a very good mood today.' Barry observed.

'Well, you got to grab every experience that is thrown at you. I must admit, I am looking forward to our little adventure today. I am sure it will be full of surprises,' Danny replied rather excitedly. 'Hopefully, all good ones, eh?'

Barry had to agree with his last statement as he couldn't deal with any more drama.

Rachael swept through the door and went straight to Danny. 'Here you are. I thought we were all supposed to meet in the lounge.'

'That's my fault,' Barry interjected. 'Danny was just getting a drink of water and we got talking. Shall we move?'

As they walked across the corridor, they were joined by Jim who had just got to the bottom of the stairs.

'So it seems we are all ready. Shall we get going?' Barry asked.

'Might as well. I did try to persuade Sarah to join us but she isn't budging.' Saying this, Jim looked towards the stairs.

Trying to reassure Jim, Barry said, 'She will be fine.'

They all shouted to Sarah, 'Goodbye, see you later.'

Sarah sat on her bed and listened to them shouting goodbye but did not respond. She waited until the front door slammed shut. When it did, she went to her window and watched as the four of them walked up the driveway and turned left. When they were no longer in sight, she moved away from the curtain and went downstairs. As she clomped her way down, she could almost see Jim glaring at her as he warned, 'Believe me, this conversation is not over.' Unfortunately for her, whenever Jim was determined to know something, he would not leave it alone until he got the answer.

She wished with all her heart that she had not come to this wretched reunion in the first place as everything was going so terribly wrong. It was a nightmare that never seemed to end.

Without realising it, she found herself in the kitchen. Seeing the glass of water left on the counter, she automatically picked it up and poured the contents out into the sink, swivelled clean water around the glass and placed it on the tray to dry. Just as she put the glass down, she noticed a bottle of red wine discreetly tucked away in the corner of the lower shelf. It looked full and yet the cork had been opened and replaced. Obviously, someone had wanted another drink after dinner and thought better of it.

She picked the bottle up and read the label. The name meant nothing to her but she recognised it to be the same one as they shared at dinner and it sure tasted good last night. She pulled the cork out and flung it over her shoulder where it bounced across the tiled floor. 'Might as well have it, things couldn't get any worse,' she muttered to herself. She lifted the bottle towards her lips and then stopped. She studied the bottle once more. It was the act of drinking wine last night that started the whole mess. Perhaps things could get a lot worse. Not wanting to risk any further embarrassments, she shook her head, poured the wine into the sink and absently watched as the blood red liquid swirled around and descended down the plug hole. Putting the empty bottle onto the draining board, Sarah wandered around from room to room.

The house was so peaceful when no one else was around. She had the whole place to herself for most of the day. Alone for most of the day... an idea sprung to her mind and she smiled mischievously. She could look around the bedrooms and no one would know. She knew almost everything about Jim so there wouldn't be anything interesting to find there and Barry was too honest to be hiding any dirty or interesting secrets in his cupboards but Danny and Rachael? Without another moment's hesitation, she ran up the stairs and straight to their door. She twisted the door knob and to her relief it opened. Obviously, Rachael was the last to leave the room as she was certain that if it was Danny, he would have made sure that he locked the door.

As she entered the room, she swept her eyes over everything. The bed was made and the room was extremely tidy. All the clothes had been hung in the wardrobes provided and extra pairs of shoes were placed in a neat row under the bed. She started poking through the cupboards which revealed just how obsessed one or both of them were about neatness. Everything was folded and placed in rows and after a while she realised that they were even placed into sections according to their colour. On one end of the drawer went the black ones and by the time you reached the other end they were white. Finding all this a bit freaky, Sarah shivered and quickly closed the drawer. She opened the next one down and noticed a wallet lying on the top of some books. She picked up the wallet, opened it and found that it was packed with various cards. She moved towards the bed and sat down. 'Who would go into town and not take their wallet?' she mumbled to herself. 'Danny, you cheapskate.'

She placed the wallet on the bed and took another look around the room. It certainly was beautifully decorated. The ceiling appeared to be higher than in her room and the walls were painted a soft shade of peach.

She saw the jug of water on the bedside table and decided to pour herself a glass. She took a few sips and then placed it back on the table. She picked up the wallet again and started to pull out one or two of the cards. There was a mixture of bank cards and membership cards. In one of the compartments were bits of scrap paper. This caught her interest and she carefully unfolded them and set them out on the bed. Each one had a name of a female next to a telephone number. One or two of them had lipstick marks and kisses. 'You dirty dog, Danny. Cheating on Rachael. Didn't think it possible for anyone else to fancy you,' she muttered to herself.

Sarah then took a closer look at the bank and membership cards, saying to herself, 'That's a bit odd.' Then, she put everything back into the wallet, making sure that all the effects were in the same place as before. Satisfied that Danny would never suspect that anything had been tampered with, refilled her glass with water and drank it in one huge swig and poured herself yet another. She did not realise just how thirsty she was after last night's wine. It had left her completely dehydrated. As Sarah drank the water, she did not take her eyes off the wallet, which was now back on the bed. Then, after putting the glass down on the table, she reached out for it again. She wanted to make sense of what she had seen on the cards. Something was not right and this bothered her. When she tried to pick the wallet up, it simply slipped through her fingers and dropped onto the floor. Sarah's hand felt numb and she could hardly clench her fist. Her vision had become slightly blurry and was feeling rather sick. She broke out into a cold sweat and started to panic. She held her hands in front of her face and saw that they were shaking, uncontrollably. Barely able to fan herself, she ran towards the door and attempted to go down the stairs. She had lost most of the feeling in her legs as well and they barely supported her as she took each step. She tripped once, twice but managed to cling onto the hand rail, preventing a nasty fall. All she could think of was to get outside for some fresh air.

She managed to get to the front door and gripped the handle in her useless hand. She was numb all the way to her shoulders and found it difficult to pull the handle down far enough to unlock the door. With all the strength that she could muster, she tugged and finally heard a click and the door opened.

Almost in tears, she fled the house, remembering that the others turned left and decided to go right to avoid meeting them in the hope that breathing in the cool air might bring her back to herself again. Sarah waddled through some bushes and found that it led to a wild garden where the grass grew thick and long. She continued to walk, stumbling from time to time and soon found herself in the forest, sheltered from the cold and damp. The ground was covered in decaying leaves and moss and looked incredibly inviting. She flopped down and was overwhelmed by the need to sleep. As her eyes began to close, she whimpered, 'Help me.' Barely conscious, a torturing pain ripped through her stomach and she started to vomit.

CHAPTER FIFTEEN

While the sun was setting over the horizon, the magenta sky was holding the sleeping clouds that drifted slowly, reflecting the remaining glow of the sinking sun. The trees had faded to grey, whilst the bushes stubbornly held on to their vibrant greens, sucking greedily on the diminishing life of the shrinking light.

There was a sense of calm that settled over the land. The red sky was like a raging fire that engulfed the heavens above, appearing to soften the icy chill to a more comfortable temperature. It was cool but by no means cold and it had not rained for the entire day.

Everything was quiet and still, even the wind had become a gentle breeze that whispered as it swept across the field, brushing the tall grass as it passed.

Four figures emerged from the side of the field and walked slowly, lazily towards the house. Now and again sudden bursts of laughter and chatter broke the silence. The four figures were not grouped together but moved in pairs, one behind the other.

'That turned out to be a fantastic day,' said Rachael, full of vitality. The fresh air together with the company of more than just Danny seemed to invigorate her. She pranced along the thin pathway with the grace and energy of a child and beamed contently. She looked so much prettier with her eyes sparkling with joy. Her cheeks were rosy and her hair was windswept. She was like a youthful spirit of nature, feeling at ease and safe in her surroundings.

'It certainly was. I cannot believe that you found that amazing restaurant Barry. I have never been anywhere quite like it,' Jim joined in enthusiastically. He too seemed much brighter.

'Yeah, it is one of my favourite places to eat,' Barry agreed, pleased by the praise.

Danny remained silent but his frown had disappeared and he had become so relaxed that he did not care what Rachael was saying or doing. At that blissful moment, as he stared up at the beautiful sky, he decided that nothing was going to bother him. He half listened to the others sharing a petty little conversation but was at peace with the fact that for once, he was not thinking of anything at all. Work deadlines could wait until Monday and bills would be paid in time. Rachael could flutter around like an idiot for now and he just felt too unperturbed to care.

'You should have bought that dress Rachael. You looked absolutely stunning in it. Brighter colours suit you,' Jim commented. His tone was light hearted but there was a tinge of frustration as he could not believe that she would forgo such an item. It was unusual and obviously a one-off. He was sure that she would never find a dress like that again.

Rachael twirled round to face him and grinned. 'Danny holds all the money and he left his wallet at home. By mistake I'm sure. Anyway, it was just a dress. Not everyone is governed by fashion like you Jim.' Once more she smiled and twirled, to face the direction that they were walking.

Danny decided to remain silent on the matter. There was no need to defend himself. He had left the wallet on purpose because he knew Rachael would want to buy something. He was not going to do anything frivolous for her and he did not want to look bad in front of the other two men. Although, deep down, he had to admit that she did look amazing in that dress.

As they got closer to the house, Jim's thoughts turned to Sarah, wondering how she was feeling. He hoped that she felt better and had not done anything stupid whilst they were away. There was no telling what she might do when a certain mood takes her. He felt guilty for leaving her and worse for enjoying the day. However, she made it clear that he was not wanted and perhaps space was what they both needed. He desperately wanted to have that conversation with her but felt it would be better to wait until after the weekend. There would be plenty of time once they returned home.

'I was thinking,' Barry interrupted Jim's thoughts, 'would anyone want dinner tonight or a simple buffet?'

'I'm still full from lunch,' Rachael exclaimed. She had taken full advantage of Danny's good mood and ate whatever she wanted. Of course, if he had said anything to her, she would have complied but for some reason he did not seem to care what she ordered.

Suddenly, Jim stopped and stared intently at the house. 'Guys, does it look to you that the front door is open?'

All of them stopped in their tracks and gawped at the house.

'I don't know, it is still too far to tell,' Rachael answered.

'Barry, what do you think? Is the door open or not?' Jim's voice began to raise with panic. His first thought was that someone had broken in and Sarah was alone in the house.

Barry stared ahead with more intensity and frowned, 'It does look like it could be open. I did lock it this morning.'

Jim did not say another word but walked more quickly before breaking into a run. The others quickened their pace too but made no attempt to keep up with Jim. He was almost at the end of the field and very close to going up the drive. The fact that he did not slow down but accelerated, indicated that there was something wrong.

As Jim reached the open front door, he ran through the corridor and straight up the stairs to Sarah's room. He screamed out her name and hearing no response began to repeat her name over and over again. He tore into her room and found it empty. His voice hitched with frustration as he turned and made his way downstairs to search every room. With every second, his hope of finding her faded. The house was too quiet and felt extremely empty.

As he looked in the lounge, the others had just managed to walk in through the door. Hearing Jim's repetitive cries, they stopped and glanced at each other. Each face was full of concern.

Barry found Jim in the corridor in a state of panic and attempted to calm him down with a gentle and soothing voice, 'Jim, it is obvious that Sarah is not here. There is no sign of a struggle and everything looks in the same condition as when we left and no obvious signs of anyone forcing their way in. It might not be as bad as it seems. She may have just gone for a walk.'

Jim gave a nervous laugh, 'And leave the front door open?'

Danny slunk behind Barry and added, 'You always said she was a scatty cow. Sounds like a reasonable explanation to me.' He grinned in his usual smug way that grated on Jim.

'Shut up or I'll punch your mouth, idiot.' Jim was now in an uncontrollable rage and lunged towards Danny, ready to fight but Barry stepped in his way, holding him back tightly by the arms.

'Come on. Sit down and we will look at this logically.' Barry was determined to defuse the situation. 'Are Sarah's things still here?'

Jim shook his head, 'I didn't check.' He breathed more deeply and seemed to be gaining control of himself. He had turned very pale and there was sweat beaded on his upper lip.

'I'll go and see.' Rachael nodded at Barry and gave Jim a sympathetic smile before ascending the stairs.

The three men remained silent and listened to the sound of her footsteps as she moved across the upstairs corridor. They heard Rachael open the door and then for a few moments there was silence. The clock in the lounge appeared more audible than usual. Each tick tock mocked their lack of patience as they waited to see what Rachael would say.

'Her bag and clothes are all here, oh and her hat,' Rachael called down to them.

'You see.' Barry felt relieved. 'So we know that she must still be around somewhere. Any moment now, Sarah might walk in and laugh at our concern.'

'And what if she doesn't?' Jim asked, with a tremor in his voice.

'We will deal with that if it happens. There is no need to be concerned yet. I'll make us all coffee.' With this, Barry went to the kitchen.

As he entered the room, he was surprised to see Danny standing by the sink with an empty bottle of wine in his hand. He was frowning and staring at it.

'I didn't realise that you came in here. You were just behind me a moment ago,' he commented. Barry was amazed at how Danny could disappear without him noticing. He was like a serpent that could quickly and silently move without being seen and turn up as if out of nowhere.

Danny shrugged and held the bottle out towards Barry. 'This bottle was full this morning.'

'Do you think Sarah drank it all and then went out?' Barry asked. Regardless of what he had just said to Jim, he could not help but to feel worried as well.

'Makes sense. She got drunk, again, and went to get some fresh air. That explains the door being left open.' Danny filled the bottle with tap water, swirled it around and then placed it by the side door. He then looked at Barry and smiled, indicating at the bottle, 'Force of habit. Too tidy for my own good.'

Barry thought about it for a moment and then nodded, showing apprehension, 'Yes, it does make sense.' He looked out of the window and saw that it was getting quite dark outside. The sun had melted into the distant fields. The soft, golden glow had been extinguished and the sky was now a burnt shade of blue. 'It will be pitch black very soon and it is not safe for someone to be out there. There are lots of sink holes in the forest, which are not big but extremely deep. Fall into one of those and you will never be found again. There is also a quarry not too far from here. Sarah isn't familiar with this place and could easily fall into danger.'

Danny leaned against the sink and folded his arms. He listened intently and then responded, 'Jim will want to search for her soon. He is already itching to go.'

'Well I can't blame him. I will have to go with him of course, I know this area better than anyone. I best get the torches. You stay here with Rachael and heat up some blankets. I imagine Sarah must be cold and tired by now. Perhaps, Rachael could make some soup or something. There's lots of stuff in the cupboard and fridge for her to choose from.'

Danny nodded but stayed where he was. He did not see the need to rush and tell Rachael to make the necessary preparations as the search would probably go on for some time before they found Sarah.

Barry wasted no time to fetch the torches. He was aware of how quickly the darkness was engulfing the world outside. There was still no sign of Sarah. It was time for them to make a move. He went into the lounge where Jim was pacing up and down, only stopping occasionally to stare out of the window.

'Jim, think it's time to start looking for Sarah,' Barry announced quietly.

Jim turned towards him with an expression of gratitude on his face. He picked up his jacket, which he had flung earlier onto the sofa and quickly put it on saying, 'I'm ready.'

Handing Jim a torch, Barry warned him emphatically, 'I lead, you follow. There are lots of sink holes and places where you can hurt yourself. Follow my path and you will be okay. Do not run off by yourself. That would be a stupid thing to do. Is that clear?'

Jim nodded but it was obvious that he was only half listening. He was fired up to find Sarah and found it difficult to pay attention to what Barry was saying to him. She needed him more than ever and he was not going to let her down. He quickly made his way to the front door and Barry called after him to slow down. Seeing that Jim had no intention of taking heed, he jogged after him. When they both reached the front door, Barry turned to Danny and Rachael, who followed. 'Lock the door behind us. It's best to keep secure. Here are the keys.' He fished around in his pocket and pulled out a set of keys that jangled as he placed them into Danny's hand. 'They are the only set I have. I didn't think to get extra one's cut.'

In silence, both Barry and Jim disappeared into the night. Danny and Rachael stood in the doorway and watched as they rapidly faded from their sight.

CHAPTER SIXTEEN

As soon as Barry and Jim were consumed by the darkness, Danny closed the door. He leaned against it as he turned to face Rachael. He could see the fear in her eyes and the slight quiver of her lips as she regarded him in total silence. Danny observed that Rachael had been acting somewhat hysterically, since the moment they realised Sarah was missing. Danny sighed, 'It's all pointless, they won't find her tonight. It's far too dark.'

A small frown appeared on Rachael's face as she said, 'They have to at least try. Oh poor Sarah.'

'God, woman, I wish you would just stop being so melodramatic. Your behaviour is embarrassing and irritating. It isn't as if you two were even friends.' Danny screwed up his face with impatience.

Rachael stared at him in disbelief. 'She is out there in the cold and dark, probably hurt. Have you no heart?'

'Well, it's her fault that she didn't do as she was told. She just couldn't stay put in the house.' Danny moved towards Rachael who automatically took a step back. He noticed this but chose to ignore it. Slowly, he raised his hand and brushed it against her soft cheek. Rachael did not move this time but stood very still. Nevertheless, he was sure that as he touched her, an expression of revulsion darkened her pallid face. He boiled it down to her being in one of her moods again. Taking his hand away from her, he passed her abruptly, calling over his shoulder, 'A woman only does well if she listens to what she is told to do.'

She turned towards him sharply and was just about to say something but managed to stop herself. If he knew how frustrated and angry she was with him at that moment, he would surely hurt her. For quite some time now, her trust and loyalty for him began to slowly erode due to his constant taunts and nasty insults. She hated the fact that he frequently misused her emotionally and more recently physically, even though she tried so hard to please him. He prodded and poked at her heart as if it was a form of amusement and entertainment. Her endurance to carry on with their relationship was not down to love but gratitude for saving her from the clutches of her partner, Bradley. So many times, when he went too far, she would lock herself in the bathroom and cry until she vomited or felt that her head would split in two. It was at those times that she wanted to hurt him and visualised herself gouging out those beady eyes or shredding his flesh with her nails. There were even moments when she believed that she could even actually kill him. Of course, once Rachael calmed down, she would be horrified with her evil thoughts and tried to convince herself that she truly loved him. She was determined to keep on believing that he was a hero, her saviour.

Now everything had changed and Rachael could no longer pretend that she had any feelings left for Danny. Closing her eyes and clenching her fists, her mind was crying out, 'You always ruined any hope of happiness for me. Just when I started to think that things were going well, you quickly destroyed it.' She was feeling that her whole world was crashing around her. She had looked forward to this weekend in the hope that it would improve their relationship and now that they were here, it only made matters worse. He could not help himself but to humiliate her in front of the others. As she watched Danny walking away, something clicked inside her head, stopping the thought of him being her saviour. She could now see the light and clearly perceive who he really was. Danny was just like all the other men in her life and she could not believe that she had fallen into that trap again. At that very moment she vowed that things would be different. She was the one who would have to change and be strong enough to take charge of her destiny. No man would ever treat her in such a vile way again. Tomorrow her and Danny would be returning home. She could wait another day or two in taking her revenge and finding a way to repay him for all the years of torment and misery that he put her through.

Danny paused half way down the corridor and spun round to face Rachael, displaying his usual dominance over her. 'Barry wants some blankets warmed up and some food prepared for Sarah, soup or anything that you might find appropriate. Go sort it out. It's pointless but do it anyway. I'm going for a long soak. Don't disturb me.'

Rachael watched as he wearily climbed the stairs. She always thought it was strange that he could go for long morning runs but found it difficult to walk up a flight of steps. She used to be concerned about his general health but now it gave her a sense of pleasure in seeing him struggle. When he reached the top of the stairs, he turned and looked down towards her. His gaze was so icy that she could feel a cold chill running down her back and his lips were firmly pressed together, forming a thin line. Rachael breathed in deeply a few times and attempted to give him the sweetest smile that she could possibly manage. She was pleased to find that it came easily, thanks to the thought of returning home and destroying his pathetic, little world. He began to move forward again until he was no longer in sight. When she heard their bedroom door close, she placed her hands over her mouth to muffle the scream that was fighting to escape. Now, she would warm the blankets and rustle something hearty to eat in the kitchen. This was purely for Sarah's benefit and not for Danny's.

As Danny entered the bedroom, he stretched to ease his aching back. His feet throbbed from the long walk they had taken that day. He sat down heavily on the edge of the bed and took off his shoes, placing them carefully by the side of the bed and then rubbed his sore feet. As he was just about to pull one of his socks off, something caught his attention. Poking out from under the bed, was his wallet. It was open and on display were all his cards and other bits of paper. In blind panic, he bent over and grabbed it, checking to see if anything was missing. All the cards were in the right place and the money was accounted for. The bits of paper with the phone numbers of the many women that he enjoyed, were still in the side compartment. He knew that he had left his wallet in the dresser drawer and would never have made such a stupid mistake as to leave it out for Rachael to see. Women could not be trusted. They all had the need to poke around things that did not concern them. They just could not help themselves.

Once more, he pictured Rachael as he touched her face. She tried to hide it but he noticed the way she shrunk back from his hand. He wondered if it could be possible that she found the wallet, looked inside and saw the phone numbers? Immediately, he dismissed it, knowing that she was too well trained to dare to open the drawer let alone look through his things.

He got up and opened the dresser. Everything was as neat and tidy as he had left it. It appeared that nothing else had been touched. That gave him some relief. The thought of someone going through his personal belongings made him shiver. He put the wallet back where it belonged and closed the drawer.

Another thought entered his mind. Sarah had been left alone in the house. Maybe she decided to have a wander around and peer into other people's things, bloody typical woman. He had left the room before Rachael and she obviously did not lock the door behind her like he told her to. Again, confused, he shook his head. Sarah had drunk the whole bottle of wine, therefore, she would not have been in any state to go up the stairs let alone look through the cupboards and drawers.

It was at this point that he happened to glance over at the side table. Something was not right. Most of the water in the jug was missing and there was still some left in the glass by the side of the jug. He knew that Rachael had not had any since the night before. Someone else must have drunk it. It could only be Sarah. If Sarah had drank all of the wine then surely she would not have drank the water as well?

He sighed deeply; there was nothing he could do about it now. He could not confront Sarah on her return because then he would be giving himself away. If dearest Rachael knew that he had been unfaithful, she would make a ghastly scene. There was only so far that he could push her and he knew that. Everyone has their limits. Danny was not quite ready for that yet.

He could hear Rachael moving around in the kitchen taking pots and pans out of the cupboards and setting them out onto the table. He glanced at the door that led to the bathroom and then back towards the door, leading to the corridor outside. He was unsure of what he should do and rubbed his chin subconsciously. 'Hell,' he muttered to himself angrily and quickly put his shoes back on. He then stood up with determination and marched towards the door leading to the corridor. Attempting to make as little noise as possible, he moved slowly and deliberately down the stairs. When he reached the bottom, he stretched his neck round the corner until he could clearly see Rachael stirring something in a huge pot. Unaware that she was being watched, she began to hum to herself. Danny raised his eyebrows and shook his head. It always irritated him when she hummed or sang to herself. Rachael was so out of tune that he could never guess what she was trying to sing. He stayed in the same place for no more than a few seconds and then, using the key that Barry gave him, opened the front door and stepped outside. He would make sure that he returned before anyone else did and Rachael would not even realise that he had left the house.

CHAPTER SEVENTEEN

The night air was turning frosty. Barry and Jim manoeuvred over the rocky terrain that served as a winding path. They had used the same path earlier in the day on their way back from their trek and were surprised to find it far more difficult to trudge along now that it was dark. Everything seemed so different, even the field appeared to be further away from the house and the forest seemed much thicker and threatening. They were both grateful for the use of torchlight that lit up the many larger stones and dips in the hardened soil. It was impossible to distinguish the variety of colour that made the landscape so beautiful. This caused the ground to be more likened to the moon with its many craters and dusty, grey sense of nothingness and yet eerie and strangely magical. If it was not for the fact that the men feared for Sarah's safety and petrified that they would find her dead, they would have found the adventure fascinating and the challenge, more exciting.

'Just remember to stay close to me and keep your torch focused on the ground in front of you,' Barry instructed. As he spoke, puffs of white vapour escaped his lips. He tried to keep his tone firm and commanding and yet, he could hear the quiver of trepidation in his own voice. Even the torch light was shaking as they stepped carefully along the jagged path. Jim said nothing but abruptly stopped walking. After a couple of steps, Barry stopped too and turned back to see what was troubling Jim. Barry then moved the torch from left to right in the direction of the path that led to the forest and then back to the path that crossed the field and into town. He scratched his head sharply and moved the torch left and then right once more.

'She could have gone either way,' Jim muttered, leaving Barry guessing as to what he was trying to say. 'I think we need to split up.' This time Jim raised his voice so that he could be heard more clearly.

'Split up?' Barry could not believe his ears. 'Have you not been listening to me? There is no way we are going to go separate ways. You don't know where any of the sink holes are.'

Muttering under his breath, Jim replied, 'Sure, and you do.'

Barry did not hear the sarcasm in Jim's voice and concentrated on the two paths. 'If you are running away from someone, wouldn't you go across the field and into town? That way you might find another person passing who could help you.'

'Firstly, the person you are escaping from might be faster at running than yourself. And how many people did we pass on the way to town today? One! It must be very rare to find anyone walking around in this direction, taking a leisurely walk... especially, after the bad weather we just had and considering how dangerous it is,' Jim argued impetuously.

'Okay, where do you think she would go?' Barry crossed his arms making the torch shine absently to his left side.

Jim thought for a moment and then explained calmly, 'Sarah is not a good runner. In fact, she tends to trip up and fall whenever she tries to quicken her pace. If an intruder entered the house, she would hide. I bet she would see the forest and go there. Actually, I'm surprised she didn't stay in the house and hide in a cupboard.'

'You know what? I was thinking a similar thing; why not just run to her room and lock the door?'

Both men fell silent. Jim bowed his head, looking sad and Barry stared out into the distance. All he could see was darkness.

'Come on then, let's check out the forest... together.' Barry moved towards Jim and patted him lightly on the shoulder with his torch and smiled sheepishly.

Jim nodded and gave a feeble smile back. His eyes were full of sorrow and Barry was pained to think that with every passing minute, hope was diminishing.

Together, they headed off towards the forest and soon found that the ground had become much softer under their feet. Before long, they were swallowed up by trees that blocked the view of the sky and made them feel extremely uncomfortable and claustrophobic. Although it seemed impossible, it was far darker than they could ever have imagined and even with the light of the torch their vision was limited. The moisture seeped under their trouser legs and into their socks.

It was slippery and before long, twigs snapped as they stepped on them and bramble thorns poked at the flesh of their ankles. They could hear each other breathing heavily as it became difficult to move their feet because of the sticky, muddy, soggy soil that they were treading on. From time to time, one of them would stumble and even fall to the ground. After only fifteen minutes they stopped, realising that they had hardly made any real progress. Jim rubbed his sore legs whilst Barry stretched his back and winced from the pain that shot through his spine.

'It's as though we've hardly moved. The forest isn't that big either,' said Barry feeling frustrated. 'I'm starting to think we should make our way back. We are not going to find Sarah tonight. If anything, we are just putting ourselves in danger.'

Jim looked towards Barry with a stunned expression. 'We can't give up now. If Sarah is left here all night, she will have no hope of surviving. The cold alone would kill her.'

'And if we continue, we could find ourselves in the very same situation.' Barry was losing patience with Jim and the hopeless task of finding Sarah.

Close by, a twig snapped.

In unison, Barry and Jim looked towards the direction of where the sound came from.

'That wasn't you was it?' Jim whispered excitedly.

'I haven't moved an inch,' Barry answered in a low voice.

Anther twig snapped louder and the shuffle of feet could be heard.

Jim's eyes widened and he shouted out, 'Sarah!' He grabbed Barry's arm and shook it firmly. 'It has got to be Sarah.' After saying this, he let go of Barry and dashed off in the direction of the sound.

'Wait! Don't run off. Jim! You idiot, wait.' Barry called after him but was completely ignored. Stamping his foot in agitation and frustration, he moaned, 'Damn!' and tried to follow him. He soon fell behind as Jim was a fast sprinter. Even though he was slower, leaves smacked Barry in the face and branches scraped through his hair and he was sure that some sharp bits of bark had drawn blood from his body. He could feel his heart pound in his chest as panic began to consume his mind. Sweat trickled down his neck and quickly grew cold, sending icy shivers down his back. Barry was furious with Jim for darting off and leaving him. He had always disliked being alone outside at night in the dark. Ever since he was a young boy, he found night time spooky and even when safely in the confines of his bedroom; he had refused to sleep without a little light from an open door or a night lamp. That was one of the things he liked about London; it never felt like night time with all the hustle and bustle of people walking about and the bright lights that flooded the streets. Now, he was alone in the forest and his mind started playing tricks on him. The trees had deformed faces with huge gaping mouths. Their outstretched branches were arms, solid enough to crush him. His eyes began to fill with tears that blurred his vision. Turning in circles, he began to whine repeatedly, 'I'm not afraid, I'm not afraid.' As he spun around, he became disorientated and lost all sense of direction. He felt like a vulnerable child again and hated himself for feeling like this. However, fear had completely shrouded all his sense of rational thought and there was nothing that Barry could do about it.

Then, the torch flickered and died.

Barry tapped the head of the torch with the palm of his hand and then switched the button on and off. His torch failed to light up.

With the little spark of determination that he had left inside of him, he began to step forward, hands waving before him and feet that felt heavy and numb. He moved cautiously, taking no more than five steps at a time. Suddenly, without any warning, the earth beneath his feet disappeared.

He felt himself falling as if in slow motion.

He must have reached the bottom within a matter of seconds but for Barry, it felt like forever. He could smell the musty, dampness of the soil surrounding him and as he crashed to the hard, stone filled ground, he heard something crack. Agony tore through his right leg and up along his spine until it pulsed, digging into his skull like sharp needles.

He screamed with such anguish that his jaw was close to breaking and he could taste blood gurgling in his throat. He pawed with his fingers against the slippery sides of the hole, his nails scraping against bits of rock and other debris. Soil tumbled into the hole from above and splattered on his head. Bits of dead leaves managed to slip into his mouth and he spat a few times to get rid of the metallic taste of rot and blood that had now mixed unpleasantly in his mouth. After a moment, he stopped and began to weep uncontrollably.

'Help me, help me, please help me,' Barry whispered over and over again. Suddenly a bright light shone before him and he could see his Aunt Lucy smiling adoringly at him. He knew that it was not possible as the hole was barely big enough to hold him and of course, she was dead. However, her presence filled him with comfort, just like when he was a young boy. He stopped talking to himself and held his arms out to her and she to him. While this was going on, someone at the top of the cavity was laughing.

★

Jim stopped running and clutched his knees as he tried to catch his breath. His head felt hot and his throat burnt like fire. He had followed every sound that he heard but was not any closer to finding Sarah. He wiped his forehead with his sleeve and began to survey the area, realising that he was lost. He had completely lost track of the various directions that he had taken and now could only hazard a guess which way would lead him back to the house. If only he had listened to Barry and not run off like a silly, little boy. In his current state, he was of no help to Sarah at all. Jim began to choke back tears of exasperation. He did not want to leave Sarah out there alone but realistically he had no choice. He had to find his way back.

Without any conscious decision, he let his feet move in no particular direction and silently prayed that eventually, he would make it back to safety.

He walked for only a few minutes and the forest began to thin out. His torch was still strong and he could see the path that he and Barry had taken earlier. He sighed with relief and chuckled nervously to himself. He was safe. He had never been so glad to see the black shape of the house grow closer. Guiltily, he turned back to the depths of the forest and whispered, 'Sarah, I'm so sorry.'

Turning once more to face the house, he put all his thoughts and energy into walking. He had to get back, he was nearly there. His life depended on it.

CHAPTER EIGHTEEN

Jim bashed on the front door as loudly as he could and cried out for Rachael or Danny to open it quickly. He could hear the faint shuffle of feet running towards the door and heard Rachael call out, 'Jim… is that you?' There was a moment of silence and then, 'Damn! Jim? I got to get Danny, he has the key. Hang on.' Then the shuffle went off into the distance.

Jim turned around and leaned his back against the door. The wood was hard and damp, pressing him in the places that were painfully bruised. In fact, his whole body ached and in the dim light, he could see sharp bits of branches and thorns that had carved scratch marks across his hands. Parts were covered with congealed blood where the wounds were trying to heal. He knew his face must look a sight as when he gently explored his cheeks, he felt similar lines etched on the surface of his skin. Some were superficial but a few had dug deep and were sore. He winced when he touched them.

As he stood waiting for Rachael to let him in, he had his eyes fixed towards the path that he had just come from and listened intently for sounds of life but there were no signs of Barry or Sarah. Not only had he failed to find his best friend but he managed to lose another one. If he had not run off, perhaps Barry would be standing next to him now, also waiting for the door to be opened. At that moment, iniquity hung around his shoulders like the weight of the dead albatross he once read about, in a ballad, years ago. Jim closed his eyes and tears began to slide effortlessly down his face; the saltiness stung as it ran over his wounds.

A heavier set of footsteps could be heard from behind the door and a key rattled in the lock. Jim moved quickly away from it, wiping the tears from his eyes with the sleeve of his jacket, which was wet and dirty from the leaves and other debris.

The door opened wide and the light shone brightly from within. Even though his eyes took time to adjust, Jim could feel the welcoming glow that cascaded over him. Some of the warmth, contained in the four walls, escaped into the open air and Jim enjoyed the way it brushed against his cold face. He could distinctly smell something savoury cooking in the kitchen and imagined something meaty and hearty, bubbling in a pot on the stove. He breathed in deeply and his stomach growled loudly. He could not believe that in such a devastating situation as this, he could still be hungry.

'God, Jim… you look awful.' Rachael was aghast by his appearance and wanted to pull him in and provide him with some comfort. She held back, only because upsetting Danny would not help the situation at all.

She was not in the mood for another argument and was not sure how she would react to another confrontation.

'So, where is Barry? What happened?' Danny asked, sounding as though he was already bored of the whole situation.

Jim stumbled into the house muttering, 'Can I sit down first?'

Rachael took his arm and led him gently into the kitchen. Danny just watched.

'I have made some stew whilst Danny had a very long shower,' Rachael told Jim and took a plate from the cupboard and started spooning the thick, temptingly aromatic mixture onto it. Homemade bread prepared by Barry earlier had been cut and buttered. Rachael took a couple of slices and placed them on another plate and put it on the table so that Jim could eat the bread with the stew.

Danny blinked when she mentioned the 'very, long shower' and hated the fact that she had to be so specific in her description of the length of time he was alone. He could see that she had said this with complete innocence and suspected nothing malicious. Jim was in such a state that he was void of any coherent thought. Danny knew that his little walk outside had gone unnoticed, just as he had hoped.

'What happened?' Danny repeated his question.

Jim was just about to put a mouthful of bread into his mouth, stopped and stared at Danny. He was pale and his expression was so full of pain and sorrow that he looked frightfully haunted. Even Danny was affected by the look he gave and felt a cold, unpleasant shiver crawl up his spine.

Averting his gaze, Jim frowned, looking down at his plate as if confused. The bread plopped down into the stew and his hand was shaking. 'We couldn't find Sarah. I heard something... ran... and lost Barry. I was lost... found my way back.' After saying this, he choked back the need to cry and buried his face in his hands.

'Now, two of us are missing, three if you count Emma,' Rachael whined.

'Don't be so stupid! Emma left, we know that.' Danny had lost all patience with Rachael and snapped at her in anger.

'How do we know that?' Jim screamed back causing Rachael to flinch. She could never get used to the sound of a man shouting. Danny never raised his voice at the start of their relationship and that was why she was drawn to him. He changed when she moved into his house and began to get constantly annoyed with her, seething, full of sarcasm and more recently violent. She rubbed her hands together nervously and willed herself to calm down.

Danny did not reply to Jim but glared menacingly at him. He was seething right now and he clenched and unclenched his hands as though he was itching to punch someone. Rachael watched as he did this and took a step back.

'Barry told us that he couldn't get her on the phone.' Jim lowered his voice trying to contain his anger.

'Probably already off with someone else. Bet she has forgotten all about him. That's women for you,' Danny said mockingly. He turned towards Rachael and his smile widened. 'Yeah, that's women all over.'

Jim raised his head and glowered at Danny. 'You really are a nasty little man.' He said this slowly and with such vehemence that Danny appeared to physically shrink back.

There was a slight pause as Danny was carefully considering his next form of attack. 'I overheard the conversation between Barry and Sarah.'

Jim screwed up his face as he was increasingly growing irritated with Danny. 'What are you babbling on about now?'

Danny knew that he had hooked Jim and he was ready to reel him in. Sarah was always a good bait to catch his attention. He stepped forward a few times and then grinned. 'That time in the kitchen, when you just missed the great confession.' He nodded his head, pleased with himself. It was clear that both Jim and Rachael were listening intently. 'Sarah admitted that she was the cause of you and your boyfriend... whatever his name was... to split up.'

Jim was wide-eyed and whispered, 'Archie?'

'That's the one. What a tragic tale it was. How he cried when he was told that it was best he walk away. Sarah told him that you didn't love him anymore. Oh, it almost brought me to tears.' His tone was becoming increasingly more sarcastic. 'She broke his heart because she was a selfish, little cow and wanted poor, ignorant best friend Jim to herself.' Danny's grin widened.

What happened next was too quick for Rachael to grasp. Jim had suddenly charged at Danny, shouting, 'You bastard!' and then flung Danny across the room. His smile was replaced by the look of shock and then pain as Jim's fist buried itself into his jaw. Rachael had no time to react until Danny had reached the opposite wall and banged his head.

Everything went silent and Jim shook his hand which was throbbing from the powerful punch that he inflicted on Danny's jawbone.

Danny grabbed his head with his right hand whilst trying to use his left arm to help himself sit up. A stream of blood slithered out of the corner of his mouth and as he attempted to grin, his teeth were stained red. He opened his mouth to say something but decided that it was not a good idea. Jim was in a rage.

'I think we should all sit down. This is getting us nowhere.' Rachael's voice was thin and reedy and yet it was enough for the two men to do as they were told. Jim nodded and sat back in his chair and Danny followed suit, reluctantly. Rachael then continued with more confidence in her voice, 'We need to think straight.'

'I will ring the police first thing in the morning. I would do it now but they won't do anything until sunlight,' Jim told them firmly. Without thinking he picked up the fork and heaped some stew into his mouth.

Danny took a tissue from his pocket and wiped his mouth with it. He had been staring at the stew on Jim's plate but took his eyes away just long enough to see the blood on the tissue. He gave a small whine and placed it in his pocket. He looked towards the pot on the stove and seeing this Rachael rolled her eyes and got up. She grabbed another plate from the cupboard and spooned a generous amount of the stew onto the plate. With a knife, she cut two slices of bread and placed them onto Danny's plate. Unlike, when she served the food to Jim, her movements were more aggressive. Danny watched her opened mouthed. He had never seen such strength emanating from her before.

'What should we do tonight?' Rachael asked. 'I won't be able to sleep anyway.'

'I guess pack. Whatever happens, we will all be going home tomorrow.' Jim had become very matter-of-fact. His mind was focused on searching for both Sarah and Barry as soon as he could. He just had to wait for the first signs of light.

Danny remained quiet as he ate his food. His jaw had started to swell up and a shadow of a bruise had begun to appear. He shovelled the food into his mouth and barely chewed it before swallowing. Danny had gone into a sulk. From time to time, he glared severely at Rachael but refused to make any eye contact with Jim.

Jim murmured, 'Sarah would never have done anything like that.'

Danny kept his eyes down but replied in a clipped, sulking voice, 'Believe what you want.'

'How did it all come to this?' Rachael was close to tears. 'How could a reunion turn so sour? First Emma, then Sarah and now Barry. We don't know what has become of them all.'

CHAPTER NINETEEN

Rachael watched as the sun began to rise from behind the horizon. At first, it coated the sky, clouds and the land below with various shades of red. The sun itself reminded her of a blood clot that dripped its moisture onto the world. The further the liquid spread, the less intense the colour became. She kept watching as the sun turned into a brilliant white. Its beams were like fingers; touching everything in sight, spreading its light on the tips of trees, bushes and even the longer blades of grass. The sky, in contrast to the sun, was heavenly and yet she felt no comfort from it.

She had not slept all night due to the gruesome thoughts that kept creeping into her mind. She did not realise that she could have such a dark imagination and begged for sleep to wipe away the many scenarios that played stubbornly and unashamedly around in her brain. She imagined Sarah shivering, her skin, a bruised pale blue as the icy wind cut into her pores. She could almost hear her weep with pain as her muscles seized up, causing intense cramp all over her fragile body. Then, she turned her thoughts to Barry who in her mind was trapped under a heavy piece of wood that pierced his skin and with each slight movement that he made, scraped against his bone making him howl with the unbearable pain. These thoughts kept going round and round in her mind and there was no way of stopping them. Rachael was tempted to clutch her head and scream them out if only this would work.

Turning away from the window, she stared at Jim who had fallen asleep some hours ago and was now gently snoring with his head slumped down on the kitchen table. Danny retired to the bedroom almost immediately after the confrontation between him and Jim but not before he had finished his plate of food. Normally, he would have commanded her to follow him but surprisingly left her sitting at the table. Rachael also found it curious that even though she had not slept all night and was feeling the strain of fearing the worse for Barry and Sarah, she felt more awake and alive than she had done in a long time. Her mind was clear and there was not a trace of a headache. She found it strange that her health had radically changed for the better overnight and under such stressful circumstances. Odd as it might seem, she certainly was not complaining about it.

She moved away from the window and stretched. Just as she was about to get some water from the fridge, she noticed that the keys were lying on the side counter. Danny must have left them there after opening the front door for Jim. Carefully, she tip-toed over to them and gently picked them up. What she needed right now was to go for a walk in the fresh morning air. Rachael was sure that neither Jim nor Danny would be waking up any time soon and she had no intention of disturbing them. The sleep would do them both good and more importantly, she preferred to spend the time alone while she had the chance. Part of her still felt scared to do anything without Danny's permission and the other part, the thrill and delight of rebelling. If I want to go for a walk then I will. To hell with Danny, she thought to herself. A smile of defiance appeared on her face with the knowledge that she would never allow Danny to dominate her life again.

She had her shoes on but decided to leave her jacket hanging on the chair to avoid disturbing Jim. It was good to see him looking so peaceful while in deep sleep because the moment he wakes up, the tension will start again.

Slowly, she stepped gingerly across the corridor to the front door and put the key in the lock. When she opened the door and sensed the cool breeze caress her face, she felt free for the first time in years. She walked quickly down the path, turning every so often to check if anyone had noticed her leaving. When she reached the road that split in two, she decided to go right, heading towards the forest. It was now daylight and she could clearly see where she was going but still kept her head down, looking at the ground not to trip over anything. She folded her arms across her chest trying to keep warm and wishing she had taken her jacket after all.

It was very still and silent with the occasional sound of birds chatting to each other in the trees. There was a sense of calm that delighted her. The space allowed her to breathe easily and her whole body to relax. Inside the house, things had become tense and strained, making the whole atmosphere unbearable; even after the two men fell asleep, she knew that it was only a matter of time before they would wake and the storm would return with vengeance.

It did not take long before Rachael reached the edge of the forest, stopping to peer inside. It was a lot darker within due to the many leaves that formed a natural ceiling. The rays of sunlight poked their way through the gaps, making the scene breathtaking. It was like a magical world that promised great adventures once you dared to step inside. The leaves that had fallen from the trees created a carpet on the ground which appeared soft and even. Due to the fact that it was so sheltered, it was warmer and there was no breeze at all. Rachael loved everything about the enchanting forest and was glad that she had been brave enough to leave the house. However, she knew that she could not stay too long and would soon, rather reluctantly, have to return.

She ambled along the path, between the huge tree trunks and lifted her face towards the sun's rays that shone down like torch light. She bathed in the heat that radiated from them. A smile spread across her face when suddenly, she felt a hand grab her ankle and with a yelp, she lost her balance and crashed down onto the ground. Kneeling just inches away from her, looking bedraggled but very much alive, was Sarah.

Rachael could not believe her eyes and froze, staring at the wonderful sight of Sarah in front of her. Her hair was matted and there were dark circles under her eyes. Her lips were dry and cracked and there were smudges of dirt on her cheeks and chin. She was very pale yet her eyes were still vibrant and clear. Although she had been in the forest all night, she looked wide awake and full of energy. Sarah looked more like a brave warrior than a feral animal. To Rachael, she looked simply amazing.

Sarah sat back on her heels and before Rachael had a chance to ask any questions, she spoke. Her voice was calm but it was clear that she was agitated and had a lot of things to say. 'Don't drink anything that Danny gives you, especially, the water in the jug in your room.'

Rachael frowned and shook her head slowly. 'Why? What do you mean? You aren't making any sense.'

Sarah sighed deeply and looked off into the distance as though in deep thought. She turned back to Rachael who watched her in silence. 'Okay. I'll start from the beginning. When all of you went into town, I decided to have a little snoop around.' She gave a little embarrassed smile then became serious again. 'I went into your bedroom.'

Rachael raised her eyebrows and looked annoyed.

'I know it was wrong but you won't believe what I found. Danny has been keeping a hell of a lot of secrets and I am sure that you know nothing about them.' Sarah looked keen to continue.

Rachael appeared to be slightly on the defensive and said, 'I don't go through any of Danny's things; he won't allow me to.'

'I can believe that,' Sarah huffed. 'Look, I am going to tell you some horrible things and you will have to listen. For your own sake, just hear me out.'

Rachael nodded her head. She had come to the point that nothing would surprise her about Danny anymore.

'I found his wallet in the second drawer down of the dresser just below the mirror. I decided to have a closer look, you know, just for the fun of it.' Sarah paused as she didn't know how to tactfully express the next thing she had to say. 'There is no delicate way of telling you but Danny has been with a lot of other women. There are phone numbers on bits of paper, some with lewd remarks that even made me blush.' She was astonished by the fact that Rachael did not even blink at this. 'Then I looked at his cards. All of them were under another name. Okay, the surname Acker is correct but the first name on every card is Joseph and not Danny. What's that all about?'

Rachael frowned again and sat up straight. 'Joseph? He has never mentioned a Joseph to me.'

'I was going to check that name on the web but then my battery ran out.' Sarah was clearly annoyed by this. 'Go and see for yourself. It might mean more to you if you look at it.'

'Why would looking at it make any difference to me? I don't know any Joseph and cannot begin to imagine why Danny would have someone else's cards, unless he's a thief.'

'Or they are actually his cards,' Sarah announced dramatically.

'But why call himself Danny?' Rachael pondered. The whole weekend was getting more and more surreal. 'What about the water? You mentioned it first of all.'

'This is when it gets really sinister.' Sarah spoke eagerly and with a sense of excitement. She shuffled around to get more comfortable. 'Whilst I was looking at his wallet, I drank a fair bit of the water that was on the side table by the bed. I think, I had a couple of glasses, maybe more and then began to feel nauseous. Everything started spinning and my arms and legs became numb.'

'You weren't well from drinking too much the night before, remember?' Rachael butted in.

'I know what a hangover is and this definitely wasn't one. I desperately needed some air which is why I came here. I only woke up a few minutes ago to find a lot of vomit right next to me. I had been sick in my sleep, many times by the amount I saw. Rachael, the water was poisoned and it wasn't meant for me.'

Rachael replied firmly, 'I had a few sips of that water Friday night.'

'And you were acting rather odd the next morning. Did you have any last night?' Sarah inquired.

'No,' replied Rachael.

'How did you feel this morning?' asked Sarah.

'Funnily enough, I felt better than I have done in a long time. I didn't sleep all night and yet I was far more alert and awake. The last time I felt that good was just before I moved in with Danny.' She gasped with the realisation of what had been going on for so long. 'I drink a bit of water every night before bed. Danny has always encouraged it.'

Both women fell silent. They had discovered something that was both sickening and terrifying.

Rachael began to panic. 'What damage has he done to my body over the years? What has he done to me?'

'I don't think he meant to harm you, just put you to sleep for reasons beyond our imagination. I assume that I had a much larger dose than you ever had and all it did was make me sleep for a very long time. I overdosed on, whatever it was and I feel okay now.' Sarah appeared very matter of fact about it but inside she too, was worried about the damage it may have caused. She just thought that Rachael had enough to deal with without worrying about her health as well. 'What are you going to do about it?' She knew that Rachael could not possibly stay with a man who was so deranged but feared the worst.

'I'll kill him,' Rachael commented angrily then frowning said, 'honestly, I really don't know. The only thing I am sure about is that I'm leaving him. As soon as I get back, I will leave.'

'Have you got anywhere to go?' Sarah asked timidly.

Rachael shook her head.

'I still live with my parents but they won't mind if you come and stay for a while. Just until you set yourself up,' said Sarah in a gentle voice.

Rachael smiled gratefully then looked towards the way out of the forest. 'I guess we ought to be getting back. I left the men sleeping and would rather get back before they wake up. Especially Danny.'

'I'm not going back. Not yet. I need a little more time away from that place,' said Sarah, grimacing.

'Don't blame you. I would rather stay here as well but I've got a wallet to look at,' Rachael sighed. 'By the way, Barry's missing. He and Jim went to search for you last night. Before you start worrying, Jim is fine but incredibly concerned about you.'

'He wouldn't be if he knew...' Sarah spoke sadly.

Rachael interrupted saying, 'He knows. Danny overheard you talking to Barry. He knows and yet still worried about you. Don't stay out here for too much longer, okay?'

Rachael got up and placed her hand on Sarah's shoulder and smiled. She then turned around and made her way back out of the forest and to the house.

CHAPTER TWENTY

Rachael's heart was pounding in her chest and her breathing was laboured as she slowly opened the front door. She stepped inside and paused to listen for any sign of movement and was relieved that the only sound that she could hear was the loud ticking of the clock in the lounge. Carefully, she closed the door, grimacing as the click of the latch seemed so much louder than usual. As Rachael crept slowly past the stairs leading to hers and Danny's room, she could not help but to hold her breath. She wanted to make as little noise as possible.

As she entered the kitchen, she glanced at Jim who had ceased to snore but was still fast asleep. She placed the keys back on the counter where she found them and returned to her place by the window. She was surprised to see that the clock on the opposite wall showed that it was nine o'clock. It seemed remarkable that so much time had passed since she set out for the forest in the early hours of the morning.

Rachael pondered whether she should wake Jim now or let him sleep for a while longer. She knew exactly how he felt about Sarah and the affect her disappearance had on him. The kind thing to do would be to tell him that she was alive and well to get him out of his misery. However, Rachael was determined to go and see for herself what was in Danny's wallet. If she woke Jim up, then she would have to wake Danny too. This would prevent her from sneaking into the bedroom and having a look inside of it. She gently tapped her fingers on the edge of the table and gazed down at Jim. He did not move at all apart from the slight rise and fall of his chest. His breathing was slow and rhythmical and his whole body was completely relaxed. This indicated that he was still in deep sleep. She remembered from a documentary she had once watched that this stage was called NREM 2. She smiled to herself thinking that at the time, she never thought that this information would be of any use to her and yet now, it was serving its purpose. If Jim is in this state then perhaps Danny might be too? Was it worth the risk? She shifted from one foot to the other agitatedly. Yes it was, Rachael thought to herself but she must stop thinking about it and act, otherwise it could be too late. At some point, Danny was sure to wake up.

Breathing in deeply, she stood up straight and began to move back towards the corridor and then slowly up the stairs. On reaching the room, she placed her head against the door and listened for any sound. All was dead silent. She could not hear any movement from behind the door, therefore, twisted the handle. Rachael felt relieved that the door had been left unlocked and opened it cautiously and peered inside. She could see

Danny laying on his front, stretched across the bed with one hand drooping over the edge of the mattress. He was completely lifeless.

Leaving the door open, Rachael kept her eyes fixed on Danny as she moved diligently towards the dresser drawer. She swiftly turned away from him and opened it. Because the furniture was new and well constructed, it opened easily and barely made any sound at all. She could see the wallet on the top and grabbed it. She turned once more towards Danny to check if he was still asleep. Satisfied that he was far from waking up, she opened it.

Just as Sarah had described, there were lots of crumpled pieces of paper with phone numbers and remarks that made her cringe with disgust. She often heard him say nasty things about loose, crude women and here he was, sleeping with lots of them. How could she have been so stupid as to be fooled by him for all those years? Of course, Rachael knew the answer to that. When Danny saved her, she was already vulnerable, weak and broken, so it was not difficult for him to enchant her with his heroic deed and demand total gratitude and devotion from her, which was exactly what he got. She was living with a stranger and all that she could think of right now was the word, retribution.

She then began to pull out the Bank Cards and even though Sarah had warned her that the name on each one was not his, it still shocked her to see it for herself. He was not just a brute but a fake.

All of a sudden a hand grabbed the wrist that was holding the wallet and yanked it behind her back. The pain shot up her entire arm and caused her to drop the wallet onto the floor. She yelped as he twisted her arm even further. It was agonising and Rachael feared that her arm would snap with the strain.

'What do you think you're doing?' Danny's hot, damp breath blew into her ear. His voice was low and menacing, making Rachael shiver with revulsion and fear.

Grabbing her hair tightly, Danny whipped her around and flung her onto the bed. He used such force that she bounced heavily on the mattress, causing whiplash to her neck. Like a rag doll, she rolled over the edge of the bed and thumped to the floor. Her head hit the skirting board and her whole body was a tangled mess. Slowly, she unravelled herself and stared at Danny; only the top half of her head was visible above the duvet. Tears ran down her cheeks and she shook uncontrollably but her eyes were narrowed to slits and filled with repugnance.

'And there was me blaming Sarah for looking in my wallet.' Danny looked psychotic as he pranced in front of her. This filled her with terror and dread as she was not sure what he would do next. Rachael did what she had always done when he was in a rage; she remained silent.

Danny used his fingers to brush through his hair. For a moment, he just stood there and glared down at Rachael who was huddled behind the duvet. He pointed at her and his next remark was chilling, not because it was threatening but because she did not expect it. 'Stay where you are. Don't you dare move. I need to freshen up. The bathroom door will be open and I will not take my eyes off you for a second.' He lowered his arm and edged his way into the bathroom. As he promised, he kept the door wide open. What could he be planning to do with her next?

From where she sat, Rachael could see his reflection in the bathroom mirror and knew that he too, could see her clearly. She watched, scared to move even an inch as he picked up his toothbrush and applied a thick coating of toothpaste onto it. He paused for a moment, stared back at Rachael, smirked and began to brush his teeth.

Rachael listened as the water gushed into the sink and the constant scratch of bristles scrubbing back and forth across his teeth. Every muscle in her body ached and her neck was stiff.

To her horror, she saw Jim warily poke his head around the door. He was sadly walking into danger and most likely, unaware of it. Obviously, he heard the sound of the thud as she fell off the bed and hit the floor and decided to investigate. Rachael wondered how long he had been standing outside the door before he opened it to see what was going on and how much had he overheard. He looked straight at the wallet on the floor and then turned to Rachael and quietly mouthed, 'You okay?'

Aware that Danny could see her every move, she tried to communicate with faint expressions and eye movements. She gave a slight nod of her head and then looked towards the bathroom. Jim studied her movements and looked in that direction.

The water stopped as Danny had turned the tap off.

Jim was already steadily making his way into the room and towards Rachael. When he reached close to the bathroom door, Rachael widened her eyes. This was done more out of panic than instruction as she was sure that if he took just another two steps, he too, would be visible in the mirror. There was no telling what Danny would do if he saw Jim in the room.

Taking heed of her subtle gesture, he stopped.

Within a split second, Danny came charging out of the bathroom. Toothpaste dripped from his mouth like the foam on a rabid dog. He snarled and made a deep growling noise and pounced on Jim. Rachael saw the toothbrush in his hand, gripped like a weapon and raised high in the air.

Everything became disturbingly surreal that played before her eyes in slow motion. All she could do was watch, dumbfounded, as Danny brought the handle of the brush down on Jim. Jim did not have any time to protect himself and with a contorted expression, silently mouthed, 'No.'

Danny's aim was sharp and the handle dug deeply into Jim's left eye. There was a wet, popping sound before blood, mixed with a clear, gelatinous liquid spurted out. Danny then pushed the brush with all his might further down into the socket.

Jim made no sound through all of this but wobbled around before flopping down onto the floor frontwards onto his face, causing the bristle end to snap, imbedding the handle deeper into his brain.

For a moment, the whole world fell into a hush and then Rachael began to scream.

CHAPTER TWENTY-ONE

'It's all your fault.' Danny sneered as he held his hands
to his ears. 'And stop screaming for God's sake.'

Rachael obeyed immediately out of fear that Danny
might do something gruesome to her and could only
look at him in disbelief. She knew that the man she had
lived with for all those years was more than difficult and
at times, extremely cruel but a murderer? It would have
been inconceivable that he could ever do such a thing.
Even though Rachael had just witnessed his brutality,
she still found it hard to accept. The whole thing seemed
unreal and she wanted more than anything to wake up
and find that it was all a bad dream. Unfortunately, this
was all real.

'I could see you pulling faces in the mirror. I
told you that I would be watching your every move.'
Danny paused, and cocked his head sideways and then
chuckled to himself, 'I suppose I should be grateful to
you my dear Rachael. You warned me that someone

was approaching. I had time to prepare myself. So, in a sense… you killed Jim.'

Rachael's eyes welled up while shaking her head in protest, sobbing quietly. Her body was huddled with her arms clasped around her knees. Jim's body was lying close to the side of her. The sight could only be described as macabre with a pool of blood circling around his head. Rachael knew that if she should somehow survive, without being killed as well, she would never ever be able to forget this day and the kind, sweet man dead on floor.

'Why do this?' she whimpered.

Danny stared at her for a moment and then laughed. 'Why? You want to know why?'

Rachael winced with every punctuated word but said nothing more.

'Where do I start?' He placed his finger on his lips and continued, 'Let me see, oh yes, the beginning of course.' Danny took a chair from the corner of the room, sat down and swivelled it round to face Rachael. 'Once upon a time, a working class couple had vowed that if they ever had a child, it would have the best possible education; something they never had. They wanted to give it a good start in life, not having to struggle financially like they did. They believed that this would be the most important gift that they could give. With the little money they had, they sacrificed everything and saved and saved in order to one day, pay for the child to attend public school.'

Rachael listened, unsure where this was leading.

'It was a huge shock for them to find out that they were expecting twins.'

Rachael's eyes widened as she thought of the name on Danny's cards.

'I think that you are perhaps beginning to put two and two together, so to speak. After they were born, the parents named them Danny and Joseph. They could not afford for both of them to attend public school so decided to send only one of them. The other, would have to go to one of the local comprehensives. They came to their decision by waiting to see which one of them would be the first to speak. They felt that it would be the most intelligent and therefore have more chance of becoming a success.' Danny smiled smugly. 'That bit was right. Joseph was the first to speak. That's me.' Danny stood up and to Rachael's amazement, stood completely upright. His sideways stare had disappeared and as he walked up and down the room, he walked with a sense of grace and confidence. He looked the part of someone from a public school.

'So, Bedford Public School accepted me as their pupil when I was seven years old and I remained there until the A Level exams. Of course, my parents were very proud with my results. They made the right choice and got value for money. As for poor Danny, he was sent to our local primary school and then secondary school. Unfortunately for him, the same one as you and the others attended.'

'So you are Joseph?' Rachael asked in a quiet voice.

'All through his school life Danny suffered. He was constantly tormented by the kids who went there because he was quiet and a bit of a loner. He wrote letters to me every week, telling me how he was mocked. On one occasion, savagely beaten by some of the bullies and how no one stopped to help him.' At this point,

Joseph stopped, overcome by the devastating account that he was giving about his beloved brother. He swiped his hand over his hair. He was very close to tears but needed to compose himself before he continued, 'I was having a great time at Bedford, surrounded by good friends whilst Danny... One day, I got a phone call from home, informing me that my brother had taken his own life. Danny waited until my parents had gone out for the evening and slashed his wrists in the bathroom. He could not carry on any longer and lost the will to live. The coroner told my parents that it was not a cry for help; he wanted to die. You see, he cut from the wrist up to the crease of his elbow several times, making sure that he could not be saved. Many veins were shredded. For goodness sake, he was only a young boy and I was not there for him.'

Rachael sympathised with the tragic story about Danny but felt nothing towards Joseph except abhorrence. She did not believe in the emotional performance that he had just displayed. How could she after what he had just done to Jim? Rachael was convinced that he was void of any feelings even towards his own twin brother.

'I vowed to get my vengeance on those who were guilty for his death. I started to reread all of his letters and one name struck me the most, Rachael. He loved you so much and yet you humiliated him by tearing the card he gave to you. If that was not enough, you laughed in his face while you were ripping it. Have you any idea how that destroyed him? He was depressed enough without you doing that to him. Do you know what the worst thing was? It meant nothing to you.'

'I was a child.' Rachael tried to explain but Joseph merely held his hand up, signalling for her to stop.

'First, I had to find you and believe me it was not easy. After getting help from a private detective, which cost a lot of money, bingo, there you were. When I saw how low you had sunk, it gave me the deepest pleasure. It would be so easy to get you to fall in love with me. Then by pure fortune, you were following your boyfriend to the alley where he was planning to kill you. There I was, your guardian angel, your saviour. I got rid of him with a quick blow to the head. Funny, I don't think his body was ever found. No one cared enough to search for that piece of scum. I guess, the rats in the alleyway found him in the shallow grave I shoved him in, behind the bushes. By the time they would have finished with him, I doubt there would have been much left of him to find.'

Rachael shivered at the thought and tried hard to erase the picture that had formed in her mind.

'At first, I wanted to kill you as well but seeing you so broken, so destroyed, I decided to play a game. I wanted you to fall in love with Danny in the same way as he had loved you. Once this was achieved, I tormented you. I enjoyed watching you suffer as I despised you. You became my source of entertainment, not in the way you might be thinking, I never touched you. The idea of having to lie next to you each night revolted me to the core. I made sure that you would sleep well so that we would never have to...' He left the sentence unfinished as the thought alone sickened him.

'The water,' Rachael muttered.

'Yes, over the counter sleeping pills are marvellous these days. I could make you sleep for as long as I wanted simply by adjusting the dosage. You can't OD on them so they were perfect for my intentions. I knew that their constant use would eventually damage your insides but that never worried me because by the time that would happen, you would be dead anyway.' Joseph paused relishing the prospect. His face looked sinister with an evil smile that would curdle anyone's blood.

'However, when this reunion came up, ah, what a godsend that was to me. Every one of you played a part in Danny's downfall and I could make all of you pay for it, in just one weekend. Emma was my first victim who I used as a part of my experiment. Ever heard of the Brazilian Wandering Spider? No, I didn't think so. Very deadly, even to humans. It is so interesting that you can buy them through the internet, if you have the money. After our evening meal and the disagreement between the two girls, I told you to go to bed while I deliberately stayed downstairs with Barry with the sole intention of getting him drunk. Whilst you were comfortably asleep, I went to Emma's room. I locked the door from the inside and then moved the wheelchair away from her reach to make sure that she couldn't get help. Then, I went out through the open window that led to the garden. Poor Emma was sleeping soundly, unaware of what was in store for her. I guess she had taken full advantage of the free wine. I opened the box in which I kept the spider and released it onto the window ledge. It was fascinating to watch him scuttle into the room. I guess the warmth inside was enticing. Obviously, I stayed outside; there was no way I was going to be in the same room as a poisonous spider on the loose. My mission was more successful than I could have ever imagined and you have no idea the joy it gave me of watching her slowly die. I let the spider run away because there was no way that I would risk my own life in capturing and placing it back into the box again. When it was over, I climbed back into her room, threw the wheelchair through the window and then her body. Once outside, I placed the corpse in the chair and wheeled it to the forest where I dumped her body into a shallow grave. It all went like a dream and no one remotely suspected that she was murdered. It felt so good.'

Rachael could see a shadow move behind the door. She quickly switched her attention back to Joseph before he noticed. She was not going to make the same mistake twice. Joseph had his back to the door and in the corner of her eyes, Rachael saw Sarah peer in and quickly hide behind the door again.

'What about Sarah?' Rachael asked.

'Now that was interesting, sometimes things just go your way.' It was obvious that Joseph was taking pleasure in explaining it all to Rachael, possibly from the need to boast to someone about the success of his plans. 'She decided to stay in and not go to town with the rest of us. Knowing how much she loved a drink, I put cyanide in a bottle of wine. When we returned, it was empty and Sarah was gone.' He frowned and paused once more. 'The only mystery is that someone drank your water and I know it wasn't you. Oh well, can't worry about everything can we?' He chuckled again and then continued, 'It was easy with Barry because he fell into one of the sink holes. How he howled as he lay deep in the ground. I couldn't help but find it funny. Of course, the job was done; I just walked away and left him there.'

Rachael thought she saw something black edging its way up from behind Joseph's right shoulder but then it disappeared. She tried hard to keep looking into his eyes but from time to time took a quick glance at his shoulder. There it was again, large, hairy legs creeping up the slope of his shoulder and edging closer and closer to his neck. By the sheer size of the spider, Rachael could only assume that it was the same spider that bit Emma. Once again, she remained completely still and watched as the creature reached out one leg and stroked Joseph's thick neck. It must have tickled him because he instinctively slapped his neck. The spider dodged the hand stealthily and bit into the jugular. Once more, it released all of its venom and then ran down the side of Joseph's arm and hid in the corner of the room.

Joseph managed to catch sight of the spider just before it vanished under the dresser. His eyes widened in panic as he realised what had happened. He clutched the side of his neck and reached out a shaking arm to Rachael. Like a drowning man, he opened his mouth to say something but sunk down to the floor. His whole body began to spasm and he cried out in agony as the pain shot through every muscle, causing cramp in each limb. After a moment, he stopped, but when he tried to speak, it was muffled. His tongue was swollen. Taking in a couple of breaths, he tried to make himself understood. 'Allergic. EpiPen in suitcase.'

Rachael did not know that this man had a severe allergy to insect bites but guessed that with the strength of the spider's venom, the reaction to the poison would be much quicker. She climbed over the bed to avoid stepping over Jim and bent over Joseph saying, 'EpiPen? You want me to go into your suitcase? But, I'm not allowed, remember? Surely, you wouldn't want me to disobey your orders after being such a good girl, in your dying moments.'

No longer able to speak, Joseph banged his fist on the floor several times.

'Where is the spider's box?' Rachael asked calmly. 'Tell me and I might get your EpiPen.'

Joseph pointed to the dresser drawer.

Just then, Sarah walked into the room and stared at Joseph as he was lying on the floor. She was very pale and her lips quivered. She turned and noticed Jim's body and a small moan escaped her lips and tears streamed down her face. She was in a state of shock and was unable to say anything at all. She had lost the one man that she ever truly loved and he died with the knowledge of how sly and nasty she could be. What hurt her even more was that she could never say sorry for the hurt and sorrow that she caused him.

Rachael knew that she had to take control and so went to Sarah and placed her hands on her shoulders. 'Sarah, listen to me. We are going to leave in a minute. We are going to leave Danny, I mean Joseph here to die. It's what he deserves. We will go to my house and after a few hours, I will call the police to tell them that I am worried about my partner who should have returned home quite some time ago. When they find Joseph, they will also discover Jim and take care of his body. The police will question us so we will tell them that we decided to leave on Saturday evening because I was not feeling well. Joseph decided to stay so you came home with me to make sure that I would be okay. Instead of going home you chose to remain with me until he returned.'

Sarah looked straight into Rachael's eyes and said, 'What about Barry and Emma?'

Rachael could not bear the thought of Barry laying in the sinkhole and Emma in a shallow grave, undiscovered and without a proper burial. She hoped that the police would be able to find them and have no doubts as to who killed them. To make sure, she went to the drawer on her side of the bed, away from Jim's body. Opening it, she took out a pen and notepad. Rachael thought that she knew Joseph's handwriting well enough to forge a letter admitting his guilt.

Sarah watched and then asked, 'What are you doing?'

'It's Joseph's confession. At least the police will know that Barry and Emma are somewhere in the forest. Damn! I don't think I can pull it off. It's not as easy as I thought. The police will know that it is not his handwriting.' She looked at Joseph and noticed his mobile phone sticking out of his trouser pocket. Grinning, she placed her hand into his pocket and pulled the phone out, opened the Sanctuary app and typed his confession on his status. She then cold heartedly looked down at him and said, 'You were very proud of what you had done. Now you can share it with other people.' She pressed send and then threw the phone onto his body.

'Are we leaving him to die?' Sarah looked towards Joseph's body, whimpering.

'Like I said, it's what he deserves,' Rachael replied angrily.

'Okay. Let's go.' Sarah began to walk towards the door, feeling unsteady on her feet.

'Wait, just one more thing to do.' She opened the dresser drawer and took out the box.

While all this was going on the spider had crept out from under the dresser, curious to see what was happening. Rachael, upon seeing it, carefully bent down and teased it carefully into the box and shut it tight. 'It's my responsibility to take control of the spider to make sure that it never hurts anyone again. Finally, she turned to Joseph, who was glaring at her. The only sound that he could make was a strained wheezing sound from his labouring breath. 'You also won't be able to harm anyone ever again. However, I will take care of the spider because it has redeemed itself and deserves full respect, unlike you. May you burn in hell.'

Rachael walked over to Sarah who was standing outside the bedroom door and without glancing back, slammed the door shut behind her. Joseph was powerless to do anything but listen to their footsteps as they made their way down the corridor towards the front door. Before the door closed, he was sure that he could hear Rachael laughing. He heard the sound of the engine starting and then the car driving off.

Lightning Source UK Ltd.
Milton Keynes UK
UKOW03f2215290317
297870UK00001B/8/P